D1473124

ZBINDEN'S PROGRESS

Christoph Simon

Translated by Donal McLaughlin

Introduced by Barbara Trapido

LONDON · NEW YORK

First published in the UK in 2012 by And Other Stories
First published in North America in 2014 by And Other Stories

www.andotherstories.org
London – New York

Originally published as *Spaziergänger Zbinden*
© Christoph Simon 2010
Agreement by Bilger Verlag

English language translation © Donal McLaughlin, 2012

ISBN 978-1-908276-10-0
eBook ISBN 978-1-908276-14-8

A catalogue record for this book is available from the British Library.

Supported by the National Lottery through Arts Council England.

The publication of this book was supported by a grant from Pro Helvetia, Swiss Arts Council.

LOTTERY FUNDED

swiss arts council
pr‫helvetia

INTRODUCTION

Reading this tiny jewel of a novel brought back my experience of watching the Theatre de Complicité's *The Street of Crocodiles*: that sense of a confined person taking wing via luminous, poignant recollections; a person sending up brief showers of fireworks from a prison yard. In this case the prison yard is a comfortable enough Swiss retirement home. It is also the declining body itself of our stalwart but grieving narrator.

Lukas Zbinden, octogenarian widower and one-time schoolteacher, is a passionate advocate of walking and has hopes of stepping out. His constant refrain, as he bends the ear of young Kâzim, the home's new community carer, is that walking is the catch-all cure against jadedness, against anxiety, against greed, selfishness and all negative thoughts. He has hopes of coaxing the young man outdoors, as he has already tried with the attendant, Lydia. Lydia has cried off as usual, pleading imminent rain and offering coffee in the day room instead. 'Coffee', Lukas informs us, is a disheart-eningly watery instant brew, for which the inmates queue up eagerly, since, having paid into the obligatory kitty, they are hell-bent on getting their money's worth.

One of Lukas's many fruitful walking recollections comes from a holiday on Ibiza with his beloved Emilie. 'Why are you walking?' asks a kindly village waiter, noting the rucksacks. 'Are you German?' While there is a slightly Teutonic texture to Lukas's walking zeal, we have our own British literary precedents in this matter. William and Doro-thy Wordsworth walked incessantly, taking refuge from foul weather behind dry stone walls; and one doesn't read far into Jane Austen without picking up that the man for Emma Woodhouse is not the alluring Frank Churchill, who rides to London for his fashionable haircuts, but the plain-speaking Mr Knightley, who enters the story knocking mud from his boots. And the woman for Mr Darcy is not the eligible Miss Bingley, who invites her female acquaintance to 'take a turn about the room', but muddy-skirted, bedraggled Lizzy Bennet, who has defied convention by striding out, cross-country, to visit her ailing sister.

An endearingly self-mocking old pedagogue, Lukas allots himself – rather as Chaucer does in *The Canterbury Tales* – the most un-gripping of group 'talks', from which the malignant Herr Imhof initiates a mass walk-out, so that even Britta, the geriatric nurse, feels licensed to join the exodus. Lukas is very good company for his readers, as his musings on fellow inmates bear witness; this, whether it be the highbrow grump Herr Ziegler, or the boozy Herr Probst, a one-time business bigwig who now pesters bemused sales assistants with a senile jabberwocky of telephoned complaints, or the sprightly Herr Pfammatter, still capable of forays into foreign cities from which he returns with a miscellany of pilfered trophies. There is also gentle Frau Dürig whose tall, courteous husband has recently been removed via the goods lift, as is the custom for the home's deceased.

These diversions are the agreeable asides along the way. What I love about this poignant story is its small, quiet quality of epic. The book is a little *Odyssey*, a little *Ulysses*; the story of one day's journey, skilfully playing in tandem with another, lifelong journey that runs concurrently as a monologue in Lukas's head. This second journey takes him on a private, grieving perusal of life with his beloved Emilie, and of his persistent difficulty relating to his son Markus. Lukas, the walker, an only child since his brother's early death, fell in love with the indefatigable, many-siblinged Emilie, by first falling for her worn and muddy walking boots as they sang out to him from the boot rack.

Emilie is astonishing in her vitality and fearlessness, in her endless, supportive soup-making for the down-at-heart, her reading groups, choirs and sewing circles, her love for Lukas and their son – and in her passion for intrepid country walks. Lukas is a city walker who loves the sight of a *chocolatier*'s window or the chance of random conversation at a tram stop, but Emilie converts him to the transfiguring joys of woodland, falcon, field and sky. And Markus, lover of the petrol explosion engine, who believes that the human heart has a finite number of heartbeats which are not to be wasted on podiatric effort – what of him? Or of his ever-anxious, pill-popping wife, Verena? Well, they are good sorts in their way. It's just that they are not Emilie; beloved Emilie who, so wholly out of character, got terminal cancer and died.

As for the one-day *Odyssey*, it is taking place indoors. For all that Lukas is ever in hope of coaxing the new assistant out of doors – possibly even to the riverbank – he is all the while leaning on Kâzim's arm; Kâzim, whose 'too shiny' shoelaces are not quite fit for serious walking. The journey upon which the pair are embarked is a descent from the retirement home's third floor and to its ground floor. It involves the precarious navigation of flights of stairs which Lukas knows all too well because he firmly eschews the lift. He knows that tread number seven is tricky, and that the worst thing about being old is the prospect of falling over. That's what got him here in the first place. He's also an expert on the differing micro-climates of levels one and two, as witnessed by the greater thriving of the potted *ficus* on level two. He knows the place on the landing where the wallpaper pattern doesn't quite match up. He recalls Pascal on the small diversions that get one through the day. He can smell the air of outdoors where hawks once sat on telegraph poles, as against the indoor overheating. But will he make it through the front door today? Or tomorrow?

Barbara Trapido
Oxford, March 2012

ZBINDEN'S PROGRESS

For lunch? Hot milk with bread. And genitalia in it. That's what Herr Hügli claimed they were, at least: some animal's genitals. He fished them out of his bowl and sat, making strange patterns on the table with them, until Frau Grundbacher and Frau Wyttenbach started telling him off. – On the bedside table? You're right, this photograph wasn't there before, there's no getting past that sharp eye of yours. Nurse Lydia noticed right away, too, when she burst into my room with a raincoat and umbrella yesterday, ready for our walk, armed against every kind of rainfall. Without being invited to, she lifted the photo for a closer look.

'Such a cheerful couple!' she exclaimed, her cheeks glowing like tiny apples, her eyes lighting up with excitement at her discovery. 'Where's that? Is that your wife? You'd think you were film stars!'

'This is the pond where she taught me to swim.' I took back the snap. 'Our son took the photo. He was ten at the time. Or eleven, maybe.'

'I didn't mean to pry,' Lydia said, apologetically. 'It's just: I've never seen the photo in your room before, and when I saw it, well, you and your wife seem so . . . '

She didn't complete her sentence. Instead, pulled the stool up, sat down beside me by the window and took my hands. And do you know what I felt? I felt you. Your warmth. Lydia's hands are like yours. And I told her about the two of us, our hazardous excursions and bold swimming adventures. How we walked along that pond beneath the trees, following the shore until no one could see us. The pond was in the shade, the sun well down. We stripped to our underwear and waded into the water. You'd put your hair up with clasps. Our son was trying to catch frogs at the shore, for poison for his arrows. You swam in the pond, showing me the movements to make. Then, in the water, you held me up with your arms and I practised drowning. After a while, I'd got the trick of it and could swim half a metre before I went under.

'The main thing's not to be afraid,' you said.

We took each other's hand and climbed out of the water as dusk was beginning to fall. At that precise moment, Markus took the photo.

Nurse Lydia listened, smiling, when I told her we wrote to each other daily for four years. – 'How are you? I am well,' and you wrote back, 'My dear fiancé, I, too, am well, and know from all your letters that you are. Would you mind writing a proper letter?'

Lydia nodded, sympathetically, when I told her about your admirer on the bird-watching course, and the storm it had unleashed in me. I told her how silent I'd been for an endlessly long day after you slapped me across the face in Bonstetten Park. I told her about how, so late in life, I started being of some use about the house, after all – and Lydia seemed just as astonished as you were, back then. Only once did I put the hoover bag in the wrong way, and all the dust came billowing out. The handle that had broken off the washing machine, it turned out, only needed some superglue. I put the photo back. Lydia offered me a coffee, in the Cafeteria, and threw the umbrella in the corner.

I love thinking about you, there's so much to remember. I can't remember a time when you weren't part of me. And these days – I don't look up into the clouds for you, I look close by.

Of course, I feel uncomfortable in this shirt – what do you think? I keep having to loosen the collar. It's mad, dressing like this in this heat, but the new civilian-service carer is waiting at the door for me, and I'd like to make a good first impression. Trustworthy. Lukas Zbinden: knowledgeable and respectable. He may always open his heart to the lonely and unhappy but, in the face of injustice, he's fearless and makes no allowances. I hope the young man might like to accompany me into town a little. That would be my greatest wish. And if I'm honest, I'd be a little miffed if he were to be in a hurry to leave again. It's always nicer if others also enjoy what gives you pleasure. Cross your fingers for me, Emilie.

Kâzim, I did catch your name correctly, didn't I? Give an ageing walker your hand, young man. I have terrible difficulty with staircases. Can you believe this home for the elderly was once a private home? That a family of just four, or five, lived here? The children would creep up to the railings, here, and crouch down to watch as their parents hosted a soirée downstairs. – Take what? You'll have to speak up. I've two hearing aids. With one, I can hear but it gives me headaches. With the other, I don't get a headache but I can't hear. – The lift? No, I never take the lift. In the lift, everyone just stands there, rigid, staring straight ahead, or with their eyes down. The door opens, someone gets out and someone else gets in – but turns immediately to face the door and study it, awkwardly. Who is it orders them all to study the door? If I have to use a lift, I like to turn my back to the door, look into the others' faces and say, 'Wouldn't it be great if the lift got stuck and we all got to know each other?'

Do you know what happens then? When the door opens on the next floor, they all get out.

I know. I ask people the most impossible questions. I ask my son to explain how the automatic gearbox works. I ask the manager, here in the Home, who knits his socks. Frau Grundbacher, do you think you're being sensitive but, in fact, are just in a huff? Herr Imhof, can you look at a cleaning lady without instantly wanting to get physical? Herr Ziegler, do you *enjoy* underestimating your ability to hurt other people's feelings? Herr Hügli, do you get up off your backside to go and see if it's raining? Or do you whistle for your tomcat to come in and feel whether he's wet?

If I head down Thunstrasse – its gentle gradient – towards Helvetiaplatz, wishing the numerous on-comers a good day, it's not unknown for someone – unsettled by this harmless act – to ask, 'Do we *know* each other?'

'No, but I'd like to learn a little about you. What spurs you on? What do you consider important?'

And sometimes someone replies, annoyed, 'Shameless idiot.'

Don't think the rejection leaves me cold. But I cushion my pain. What a pity, I think, making allowances, that he doesn't feel like getting to know me. If I see him again tomorrow, I'll give him another chance.

Who do you have to thank for ideas, Kâzim? I like to eavesdrop on conversations in the street. Expressions of affection always trigger a smile in me. I listen especially attentively if the voice in question sounds troubled. For ten minutes, I can be dragged through the abysses of life, to continue afterwards, grateful for my own good fortune. My wife, may she rest in peace, didn't like that. She'd say, again and again, I shouldn't need the stories of strangers, snippets from other lives, to give myself a boost. I told her once, while it was still fresh, about a phone conversation I'd overheard – an excited French-speaker at the station, whose Saint Bernard bitch was locked in his car, in the car park of the Dog School in Lausanne – and when I started to stutter and lose my thread as I tried to repeat the scraps of French, Emilie just said, calmly, 'You're getting lost in the detail, Lukas.'

This is the sixth step, if I'm not wrong. A splendid step, isn't it? The next step is number seven on the way down, eighty-eight on the way up. Immaculate, isn't it? – Please, why do you think I keep putting my hand behind my ear and shrugging? You have to speak up more, Kâzim. Speak slowly and clearly. – Thank you, it's hardly worth mentioning. At a leisurely pace, but it's possible. Apart from when I put my weight on the wrong hip.

17

Last Wednesday morning, I was walking around the local area here. That early in the morning, no one feels like a conversation, apart from Bobby who distributes the free papers at the tram depot. Once, in the snow, my feet slipped away from under me, I fell on my back, and Bobby helped me up again, saying, 'A less agile old man would surely've got a broken neck.' With this flattering remark began a casual friendship that both of us cherish.

I sit down beside him. The pile of free papers he's supposed to be handing out is on his lap. I inquire about his well-being; Bobby, bleary-eyed, inquires about mine. Then he asks if I'd like a paper 'for the tram'.

Bobby's dressed the way, in his opinion, someone doing his job in early summer should be: trainers, jeans, baseball cap, a windcheater, to which his ID is clipped.

'People aren't going to come up and snatch the paper from the hands of a seated distributor,' I say.

Bobby sighs.

'Give me the rest. I'll hand them out in the Home. There's your tram coming.'

'That's good of you, Herr Zbinden.' Bobby raises his baseball cap and calls back 'Thanks', over his shoulder.

The stop empties, the tram drives off. Then the stop fills with people again. A girl sits down beside me: a girl with braces and a school bag and dangling legs. I ask would she like a paper 'for the tram'. The girl declines, politely. She doesn't read newspapers, so I ask what she normally reads. Then I wait: I can see she's examining me, taking her time before she answers. I'm dressed the way, in my opinion, someone going for a walk should be: a sailor's cap; a tucker bag with tassels; shoes, badly worn at the heel.

'I like reading fairy tales best,' the girl says, finally. '*Hansel and Gretel* at the moment.'

'Breadcrumbs were supposed to lead them home,' I recall.

'The witch gets burnt to cinders,' the girl says.

'Do you like school?'

'I'm good at Arithmetic and Writing. Really fast – like a machine. I'm top in GIS too.'

'What's GIS?'

'No one knows, exactly. To do with maps.'

'I used to be a teacher. GIS didn't exist in those days. What age are you?'

'Eleven. And you?'

'Count the wrinkles on my face. Like the rings on the horns of an antelope.'

'Do you know what I want to be when I've finished school? I want to have a jewellery shop in every single country in the world.'

'Every single country in the world? That's great!'

'Maybe not New Zealand. I've nothing against New Zealand. We were there last year. But it's too far away for a jewellery shop. What are you doing with all those papers?'

'I want rid of them.'

'Give me a few. I'll hand them out at break time. There's my tram coming!'

'That's really kind of you!' I raise my sailor's cap and shout 'Thanks!' as she walks away.

A businessman sits down beside me, and for the next ten minutes fends off my questions. Would he like a *Gazette* 'for the tram'? – a hand waves it away. What his favourite subject at school was – a suspicious look. Why, in his opinion, New Zealand is avoided by jewellers – he moves away, as if I'd something contagious. Whether, professionally, he'd made it to where he'd dreamed of as a boy – he stares straight ahead. Many I encounter find it difficult to come out of their shell.

Today seems quiet, at least. Other days, activation therapists and nurses in white tunics and great-grand-children whizz past at such a rate, you have to cling to the banister as you would a ship's rail when huge waves crash on board.

Listen, Kâzim, I don't want to keep you back, but would you do me a favour, young man? Would you accompany me on a walk outside? I know you've lots to do, but I assure you, you won't regret a walk! Precisely *because* you've lots to do. Walking is the oldest form of mental and physical exercise. Adam and Eve walked out of Paradise. Socrates strolled along a newly inaugurated street on the look-out for curly-haired boys to kick. Jesus and the Devil took a walk in the desert and, inspired, talked shop. Eighty-seven-year-old Lukas Zbinden may no longer be strong enough to pull a plough; not wanting to plummet into the void, he does a recce before each step; still, he strides along the street undeterred, avoiding its many dangers, like Moses through the Sea of Reeds.

I give an example that contradicts the view, very prevalent here in the Home, that old people would surely suffer heart attacks were they to subject themselves to the exertions of a walk.

What is granted, do you think, Kâzim, to those who go for walks? Incredible *joie de vivre*, that's what! Happy – in a way that's almost laughable – relationships! Incredible solutions to problems of Physics! Icelanders walk, naked, in the snow – and manage to maintain their body temperature without ever breaking into a run. And do you know the best of it? Out walking, you could meet a partner for life, one who won't want to marry you just for tax reasons and your pension.

As a young man, a trainee teacher, I visit the home of a fellow student. Before the shoe rack is a pair of – muddy – high boots. When, furtively, I lift them, I see the sole's almost completely worn out. I put the boots back and later – it's a big family – ask, 'Whose boots are those?'

'They belong to our Emilie.'

We look at each other – and in no time engagement rings are being exchanged.

But will you accompany me outside, Kâzim? Into the fresh air?

I have to tell you: I'm a social animal, not a loner, I like to have company when I go for a walk. For many, being alone may be the point of a walk. They don't want to have to bow to others, prefer to walk when and where they please. They don't want to hear other people's commentaries on views; they're unsociable. Herr Ziegler, for example, in Room 219, will protest, defiantly, 'One walker is a walker. Two walkers are half a walker. Three walkers are no longer a walker at all.'

Have you already come across Herr Ziegler? He says hello to no one, and wouldn't thank you for saying hello. He's not in the least interested in meeting people. A small, dry figure who makes his way around the Home careful to keep at least two steps between him and anyone else. His head's always lowered a little, as if he's just solving the last mysteries of humanity – the origins of the Nazca Lines, the significance of the stone heads on Easter Island and the crop circles in Wiltshire. On a mild day, he'll sit down on a remote bench in the courtyard with an archaeology book, and if I join him and start to speak, he'll clap the book shut and get up and go, without a word in reply. He frightens me a little. His wife lives not far from here, in *Domicil Elfenau.* For reasons you're best not asking about, they wanted to be assigned to two different homes. You can believe me when I say this, though: at least occasionally, even lone wolves like Herr Ziegler like to go for a walk with someone else, or as part of a group of like-minded people. As you know: no one is so perfect as not to need someone else to point out a charming bed of red carnations on Florastrasse, or a delightful little wind from south-south-west up on the Gurten, or a sleepy sawmill in Bümpliz.

The person waiting for the lift back there is Herr Furrer. Former engineer. An open, broad-minded man, and much more friendly to you civvies than Herr Ziegler, say. He'll take the greatest pleasure explaining to you how the fountain in the courtyard works.

Among the advantages of walking in company is that it's not so easy to accost *yourself*. That's especially important for walkers who are easily distracted by their own thoughts. Those who brood over the slights suffered at the Police Headquarters on Waisenhausplatz, and so crash straight into the hapless pensioner who chooses that very moment to shuffle his way round the Oppenheim Fountain.

Take two sociable country walkers – my late wife and me: we experience, together, the shift from colourful natural meadows to shady pine forests. We talk about the upheaval in the last Ice Age when the glaciers pushed way beyond the borders of our cantons, creating prominent moraines. Emilie describes the din of the massive rock slides that filled the valleys with debris when the glaciers retreated, and suddenly we're back in a vast moor. We walk along narrow boards, half submerged, jumping from one firm patch to the next. The boggy ground beneath our feet squelches, sometimes, and gives a bit. Wooden crosses mark spots where someone lost their footing and got bogged down, but what's Nurse Alessandra doing there, in the corridor? Why's she crawling around on all fours? Come along this way, Kâzim. Alessandra! You see, she'd like to run off, but she's kneeling on her tunic.

Nice to find you here, Alessandra. What are you doing on your knees? Don't you feel well? – Pardon? Well, what if you were maybe to squeeze your hand in carefully, who knows? Have you met this young man already? Our new civilian-service carer, it's his first week here. His name is Kâzim. Side by side, we're taking the stairs, one at a time. – Correct. You said it. A substantial part of my life takes place on this staircase. I've passed this plant so often, I can already call her a close friend. – Good question, Alessandra, I don't know, do you like it so far, Kâzim? – You should try to feel at home here. It's not half as bad as you imagine, maybe. Perhaps you're a little afraid, I was the same. The first time I stepped into the entrance hall and saw all the old people, I'm telling you, I felt quite scared. Alessandra, what if you were to get back onto your feet? You could join us. – No, no, don't let us disturb you then. See you later! Back to the staircase, Kâzim.

No doubt you'll soon take a shine to them all: the respectable ladies and eccentric gentlemen, the talkative widows and the taciturn bachelors, the seasoned walking-frame users, shuffling stay-at-homes with faces like dried meat. The confused ones, whose thoughts roll around like peas on a plate. Those on medication, with a cocktail in their veins of which blood's just a minor ingredient. Veteran engineers, tradesmen and -women, office workers, housewives, civil servants, army personnel, fire extinguisher inspectors, bus drivers, over-achievers, service workers, stationery shop staff. People who started allowing themselves a holiday only once it became a legal entitlement. Therapists and kitchen staff. Great-grandchildren that are always skipping two or three steps. Nurses, with a resident in each hand, leading them to the lift, taking the trouble not to forget we had a life before we moved here. Anxious sons and daughters who – on an excursion to the mountains – phone the management here and ask them to keep an eye on the money their elderly relatives have with them.

I was sitting in my room, yesterday, on the stool with the woven seat, waiting for Nurse Lydia who had promised me a walk to the Zoo. She comes in, still wearing her cagoule, and says, 'Herr Zbinden, the walk's cancelled. We're going for a coffee, in the Cafeteria,' and, linking her arm in mine, pulls me to my feet.

'I don't mind rain,' I say, shuddering at the thought of ordering a coffee, only to be given a Nescafé. For which, by the way, we all pay ten francs a month into the kitty. At ten in the morning, the place is always full to the brim with people trying to get their money's worth without dying of heartburn.

So I put my cap on and leave Lydia to Frau Rossi, who needs pushing to the Prayer Group. – Tired? At Lydia's age, you aren't tired, Kâzim. – The air? The air here in the Home, you mean? That's what makes Lydia tired? If Lydia were to go for a walk and have to avoid all the umbrellas put up by visitors to the Zoo, she wouldn't have the time to feel tired.

I then had a rather long way home ahead, carrying my tucker bag with unused umbrella in it, to boot. The benches in the Zoo were long out of sight, there was no market square decked with flags to rest in, and the only person to pass by was a young, maybe forty-year-old man.

When he got close enough, I asked him would he do his good deed for the day and carry my bag for me? He took it without a word, then, after a few steps, he took my arm too, and, a few steps further on, he ordered me to 'Stand still and take a deep breath!'

I did what I was told, which he clearly liked, for, every few steps, he repeated his command. Though I got my strength back, he insisted on accompanying me to the Home. Which was where I wanted to go. In reply to his question – what the most difficult thing about old age was – I answered, 'Falling down.'

You trip, Kâzim, you lose your balance. You get up out of the armchair, feel your knees give and fall on your belly. In a few decades, you'll fall down too, there's no avoiding it. Old people fall easily – my brother-in-law Ignaz, while putting out his organic waste; my grandfather while jumping off a tram. It's a great temptation just to remain seated wherever you sit yourself down. Let me tell you how dangerous that is. That can very easily be the end for a walker. Herr Feuz, Room 302, has got into the way, instead of standing up, of greeting a guest by simply saying, 'You don't mind if I remain seated?'

Of course, no one is cruel enough to reply, 'No – kindly get to your feet', and yet that's what you should do, for the person's own good.

Apart from this battle against falling too frequently, I don't take my frailties all that seriously. Losing or misplacing things, spilling something, forgetting a lot. How I put on my coat now is very different from what I did a year ago, and more than once I've left my bag lying somewhere. As an old person, however, you shouldn't think you're any less important than when you were younger. Emilie always said the one really essential thing was to remain lively, active and interested, and always open to whatever's going on both in nature and within oneself. We could talk much more about that, Kâzim, if we went for a walk.

My wife was a keen country walker, I should tell you. Emilie liked dizzying heights, old wooden bridges, scenic pastures and orchards on riverbanks. Intuitively, she'd abandon paths and climb up stony rocks that offered a view of yellow fields and the hills all around them. She liked gravel banks, how their whitey-grey patterns served as camouflage for the nests of little ringed plovers and sandpipers. Emilie's sharp eye made nonsense of every camouflage. Her eyesight was astonishing. Right up to the bitter end, she could discern motionless birds – invisible to my eye – in trees and shrubs in the local nature reserve. It always pained Emilie if a hollow was filled up with building rubble, a path was tarmacked over, a wooden fence replaced by metal railings. If elderly barns gave way to a car park, or the edges of forests and streams were rectified. Or mountains, once craggy, now levelled off.

Emilie! She had a thin face, red from the sun, eyes that were level when they rested, a pointed nose, and she was lean as a lamb. The daughter of a forest nurseryman from Ostermundigen. I tell you: she was full of vim and vigour.

Had we not married, I'd have chased her all my life. Careful. There's a wonderful creature at your feet. What's a caterpillar doing here? Did the smell attract it, floor wax with a hint of limonene? – Pardon? Don't mumble to yourself like that, Kâzim. But yes, onto the *ficus*. Good idea. Do you think the Home smells odd to visitors?

I'm maybe a sociable, but not a really *keen* country walker, I have to admit. Crossing monotonous meadows or exposing myself to ticks in the forests is not my thing. A horse out to grass isn't something I'd notice. Only when bridled and decorated and in a parade would it have my full admiration. Emilie liked trees standing randomly in a landscape; I like trees in rows. I've nothing against cow pastures being built on, even to be replaced by hangars and shopping streets providing free entertainment. I *yearn* for tranquillity, but can't actually bear it.

Emilie used various means to tempt me out of built-up areas. She'd turn the radio up, ask an incomprehensible question, and I'd nod in agreement. Once out and about, she'd explain the fascinations of nature to me – while, for her sake, I was happy to be bored.

'Do you see, Lukas,' she might say, 'the fir tree might not have much time for leaves, but it's green, nonetheless, from top to bottom . . . Not every bird migrates to Africa . . . And now I'm going to show my husband the last dewdrop falling from the last green leaf on the last branch of the last tree on earth . . . '

Grumbling, I walked along forest edges, counting the paces. After a country walk, I generally thirsted to do something technical, something very clearly unnatural. So I'd climb on a chair and clean the extractor fan.

Often, I accompanied Emilie to ensure she didn't roam alone. Once, Emilie was out and about on her own in the Simmen Valley, when a Mercedes stops and an arm waves out of the window to her. She goes over to it, expecting maybe long-lost relatives, but finds there's no one in the car she knows. 'Would you like to go swimming, young lady?' a voice from within asks, opening the passenger door, invitingly. 'I've just driven past a splendid little lake, fifty metres back.'

If you're married to a country walker, you fear on a daily basis she'll be brought home in eighteen blood-soaked bags.

I don't know how the climate conditions vary from floor to floor, but the difference between the *ficus* on the ground floor and this one, above the second, is striking. – This one grows better, much better.

Have you already introduced yourself to Frau Beck, of the cleaning team? She mops the floor, wipes my shelf, hoovers my carpet, airs my room, and I make the time pass more quickly by telling her about the things going on around her. Frau Beck replies, wearily, 'Oh, Herr Zbinden, you and your constant talk about going for walks. There's no accounting for taste, they say. The same must go for hobbies.'

'Frau Beck, you amaze me. Going for a walk isn't a hobby! Do you know what it means to go for a walk?'

She rushes off with my dirty washing before Zbinden the Walker can enlighten her.

Do you know what it means to go for a walk? Going for a walk is: acquiring the world. Celebrating the random. Preventing disaster by being away. Speaking to the bees though you're already a bit too old for that. Not being especially rushed on a street that's like an oven in the afternoon sun. Missing the tram. Remaining within earshot of gloomy lads whose voices haven't completely broken yet. Reading, with Bobby, the skid-marks left in the snow by people who slipped. Going at your own pace. Going for a walk is: saying hello to more people than you know. Losing Frau Dürig amid the turmoil of the Christmas Market. Sensing a storm brewing, from a distance. Avoiding damage to property. Being amazed at how much you can cut away from a tree without killing it. Having to become aware, together with Emilie, of the planets above us. Going for a walk is: always wishing for a little more than a walk can offer, but never wishing it *so much* that you get discouraged. A walk can cure a troubled soul and a broken heart. The door's open; step out and be blessed.

Be blessed, I know – that's not what you want to hear. To you, it sounds ridiculous, doesn't it, young man? Once I was crossing a bridge, the Kirchenfeldbrücke. Two men, one youngish, the other older, were outside the Casino. As I walk past, the older of the two greets me, 'Good afternoon, Herr Zbinden!'

Now it's my turn to ask, 'Do we know each other?'

He laughs and explains to the younger one, 'This is my former teacher. Herr Zbinden. A very decent teacher, he was.'

'Samuel!' I exclaim. 'Samuel Klopfenstein! You were late for everything!' – and I'm amazed that, even in a small country like Switzerland, twenty or thirty years can pass before you happen upon your former pupils.

'In case the chalk was all in the sink, Herr Zbinden always carried some with him. Three white pieces, one blue, one red. Wasn't his only quirk.'

'My only what?'

'Really, Herr Zbinden. You were a very decent teacher. But you were always talking about going for walks.'

'Heavens,' I exclaim, radiant. 'That isn't a quirk!' I turn to the younger of the two. 'I assume you have an occupation that eats all your time. And two children are waiting at home for you. Imagine, you're trying to read the instructions for a new camera while little Diana's insisting, vociferously, that you look at her picture book with her, *Look – what's that crawling there?* – and little Bruno's poking his fingers in your eyes to see if you're alive, still. At that moment, everything depends on whether or not you've secured your own space, one that isn't a brandy cellar. At that moment, everything depends on whether you go for walks or drink yourself to death. Do you go for walks, young man?'

'You see?' the older one says, smiling at the other. 'There he goes again.'

Look at my shoes, Kâzim. Tanned leather soles, double-stitched. Inside the Home, I wear simple slippers. If I go for a walk in the courtyard in those slippers, I keep losing them. What do we conclude from this? That, outdoors, human beings instinctively step out more energetically. When my unassuming grandmother went for a walk, she wore shoes she could put on either foot, left or right. Indeed, she *had* to do this. For them to wear evenly. – Brandy cellar, here? You're joking, Kâzim, there's no alcohol here. A quarter-litre of wine at mealtimes is all that's permitted, and the warden ensures that's kept to. Herr Probst's secret trips to the kitchen storeroom are the result – to top the wine up with kirsch. How long after breakfast is still too early for a glass, Herr Probst? Who have you to thank for your alcoholism?

Even if my legs are feeling wobbly, I go for a walk. Even if I feel no desire whatsoever to go for a walk. How you feel before a walk is often in reverse proportion to what you will gain by walking. The worse you feel, the more wonderful the walk, maybe because ill humour increases the body's adrenaline production. I didn't leap for joy, exactly, any time Emilie suggested – despite the rainy weather – looking for hawks and falcons at the military airfield, but I always did look for my walking shoes. Hawks, falcons and sparrowhawks, I should tell you, used, in the past, to be perched on every telephone pole. For years, Emilie blamed her powers of observation for their disappearance. Until she realised that, quite simply, they were no longer there.

Is this too slow for you, going down the stairs? Just say, if so. You don't need to claim, out of pure charity, that you *like* walking slowly.

•

You see, I'm weak when it comes to staircases, but I don't say 'I will not fall' for the thought of 'falling' is more likely to cause a fall than the force of the accompanying 'not' is to prevent it. I tell myself, 'I can walk safely on stairs.'

If you intend avoiding the sniffles, you don't say 'I'm not going to catch a cold' but 'my mucosae are functioning perfectly, my immune system is my shield and protection at times of peril, I am secure, unassailable, within it'.

If you don't fancy going through the woods for fear of meeting a bear, you say – but look who is coming towards us! Frau Jacobs, everything okay? – You're in a hurry, I see. – Visitors? That's nice. – Oh dear. Well, put some milking grease on it. That will stop it itching so much. – Definitely! Get Lydia to give you some milking grease! – I don't know the Gurtners, do I? – Aha. Yes? – Really? – And how. – Why, yes. – This shirt, you say? It's to create a good impression, nothing more than that. May I introduce our new carer? Kâzim; his hair curls despite everything he does to stop it. – But no, please, don't let us keep you back. – If you go up a floor, don't go falling over Alessandra. She's on all fours, looking for Frau Binggeli's crown. – And get Lydia to . . . Exactly!

A feisty lady. Did you notice that when Frau Jacobs laughs, her face completely changes? Her eye area breaks up into a thousand little crinkles and she bares two rows of immaculate, snowy-white false teeth. Never again, she once announced, triumphantly, would a dentist discover a problem with one of her teeth. – Oh, I know. You were told Frau Jacobs is always complaining. That a blouse she didn't like was put out for her. And the drama with the eye drops. – Naturally, Kâzim. But Frau Jacobs hits Lydia because she gives her the eye drops just as she's waking up and is still half-asleep. – Of course. Ask for yourself. I stick a leg out sometimes too when Lydia bursts in, asking for an arm. Not always easy for the nursing staff, we old fools. But to return to the bears: let me reassure you. The likelihood of encountering a bear while out for a walk in the woods is minimal. As long as you avoid clumps of bushes with berries, don't follow bear tracks and tie a bell round your ankle. – You're not afraid of bears? – Of dogs? Never look a dog in the eye.

A sociable walker like me gets to hear excuses from all kinds of people. My son, who has turned grey too now, claims walks are for pensioners. They eat up your time. No one else goes on them. Engines exist for those purposes. He's not attractive enough, he says. Or has better things to do. You can fall over. According to him, going for a walk involves meeting people you can avoid by staying at home. You've sore muscles the next day. Blisters on your feet. You're at the mercy of the weather and all the dirt in the wind. The human heart is programmed to beat so-and-so many times, he says, and you die when you use your last beat. Every activity that increases your heartbeat should therefore be averted. 'Father, you just want to put me off driving,' he says.

My son as a driver: one hand on the wheel, the other dangling out of the rolled-down window. His watch, temporarily on his right wrist so the white patch on his left can also tan. His concerns, if you urge him to go for a walk, are truly unusual. His face rigid and pale with displeasure, it's as if he were asking, 'How long might it be before I actually get somewhere? What could go haywire at home while I'm being idle, out for a walk? How am I supposed to pay the bills run up while I'm out?'

You reckon he shouldn't be so docile, allowing himself to be inundated by doubts like that? What I always say is: one of many entertaining ways for a motorist to ease his way into the flow of pedestrians is for him to go in rolling a car tyre along, and using a square-section key. If several motorists join in at once, one of them can give his tyre a push, and the others can try to throw their car keys through as the tyre trundles past. You laugh! But the truth is that no one can ever get my son out of his hermetically sealed spaces. Should he, one day, step outside and actually walk past his car, bells will ring to tell the world a miracle is happening. – My son's profession? Biochemist. In a lab that doesn't tax him too much. He told me once, 'I created a bacteria strain, then spent the whole morning watching a Scania trying to turn.'

I can imagine what's going through your mind. The answer is: no, I've nothing against motorists. Why should I? They kill themselves to be polite to me. If I'm standing at the zebra crossing at the Freudenberg *Migros*, the traffic on the slip-road to the motorway will come to a standstill while one driver stops and waves me across.

If my son collects me for a father-and-son outing to Emilie's grave, I – conscientiously – practise being a passenger. It's an art form. I look in the mirror on the back of the sun visor and pull funny grotesque faces. I look fierce and wild; smile sweetly. Like a child larking about. I lean forward and look through the windscreen and discover – in the clouds above Mount Niesen – half-boots and contrabasses; a rotting mummy; a bloated sheep; the profile of a talking head. If the sky is cloudless, I'm pleased about the good opportunity the sun is getting, and report where the rays are falling to my son. 'On the left, the sun's shining into a shed in Hünibach and tickling a pig's ear so much it needs to sneeze. On the right, the sun's shining onto the Park Hotel, which is slowly desiccating and shrinking.'

My son's an expert on the many colourful cars that drive past. As a child, he cut all the cars out of glossy magazines and brochures: the Cadillacs, Buicks, BMWs; the posh Borgward Hansas; the Chevrolets; the Opel Kapitän limousine; the improbably long Oldsmobile 98 Convertible. Nowadays, he can still identify all the different models and, if I'm in his good books, he teaches me too. If, concentrating hard, I look for a few minutes at everything whizzing past, then close my eyes, he asks me questions like 'How many silver Citroëns were parked outside the St. Beatus Caves? Which turn-off did the red Datsun with the tinted windows take?'

'Look at these.' In the parking space at the cemetery, I lift my feet onto the dashboard. 'Do you know what these are?'

'Feet,' Markus answers, emphatically, calmly.

'And what, do you think, do we need them for?'

'The left one for the clutch. The right, for the accelerator.'

Markus claims he can identify cars blindfold if they're parked and creaking irregularly as they cool down. A talent that can't be explained in terms of his immediate predecessors.

Do you have children, Kâzim? We don't need to discuss that in depth right now, but if you give a child a rain cape as a present, instead of a pedal tractor, it will be able, one day, to do without a car.

Whereas I've come to understand how wrong people think I was, the way I tried to rear my son to be a walker.

I drag him away from his chemistry set. Emilie's already standing there, holding his cape.

'No!' Markus roars. 'I simply can't believe I'm supposed to join you on this frigging walk with the Nägelis! The Nägelis are *your* friends, not mine!'

'It's nothing to do with the Nägelis, it's to do with your friends from the playing field.'

'What about them?'

'It's to do with you taking penalties with Lisa Stoll's dolls.'

'I'm telling you a-bloody-gain: that's not true. What arsehole made out – '

Enter Emilie: 'You'll come with us until you learn to speak to your father in a different tone.'

'I must've been adopted! My real parents would never treat me like this!' He has paled with rage, his voice cracks. 'And I won't be putting this damn cape on, that's for sure. It's for kids!'

'My brother died of pneumonia at your age!' I hurl at him. 'And I've no desire to see the same thing happen to you.'

We all have sensitive spots that we can't bear to be touched.

'If you've children of your own one day,' Emilie says, in a more conciliatory way, putting the cape over our son's head, 'then you can do things better from the outset.'

At the Steindler schoolhouse, I often heard it said with a sigh that you should have your own children – because those were the only children who would really have any time for you. There were times, with Markus, when I strongly doubted that. 'Having a teacher as a father is real bad luck,' he often said when fellow pupils, who should actually have been his friends, had pulled his swimming trunks off in the beginners' pool, or excluded him from listening to Elvis Presley. Do you think too, Kâzim, that your parents should never have parented?

Of course, the world was different back then. When it came to discipline and the way things should be, I had a less relaxed attitude than my son has nowadays. Sit up straight. And eat up. Don't crawl around in the dirty washing. What's the magic word? First, tidy your things away and put your pyjamas on. I thought we'd agreed you don't point arrows at people? Fingernails aren't a type of food. If he was given too many Christmas presents, half of them would be locked away and kept for the following year.

I'd always feared that if my car-daft son ever had to decide between saving a child and saving a vehicle, he'd crush the child in the gutter. And yet Markus observes speed limits very carefully; never crosses the white line in the middle of the road; doesn't have a go at pensioners, puttering along in their Porsches; and he's turned out to be a wonderful father. I remember all the photo albums in the bookcase at his place. I take one out and it happens to be a record of the seventh year of my granddaughter's life, with the funny things children say about starting school and birthday cards in between the photos. I say, 'Verena gave herself a job, doing all this.'

And my granddaughter, quite astonished, answers, 'No, Dad did that.'

Emilie wasn't a member of the Women's Movement – the Suffragettes and the International Women's League for Peace and Freedom – but she taught Markus how to iron and sew buttons on, and where the antiseptic is kept. Quite deliberately: I'm showing you this so you never have to be served by a woman.

At Advent, I would pull myself together, fetch a few branches from the garden, pin an arrangement on the front door, help to put up the Christmas tree, put an apron on and knead dough. Every evening, I'd end up with a sore stomach – from raw almond dough.

Once, when Emilie was out, the little smart aleck said to me, 'You know, now Mum's away, I could do everything for you that she does.'

I'd already given him his pocket money, though. This reckless action on my part meant he'd no incentive.

Have I mentioned this already? Going for a walk is: finding out who you are and liking what you discover. I'm a gentle walker. A person who, after the storm and stress of my career, a marital triumph and a paternal defeat, has regained my inner balance.

Were the earth to be populated only by gentle walkers, there'd never be any crush, or pushing and jostling, any disregard for right of way, or digs in the ribs; resounding slaps would happen only as a preventative measure. Would you like an apple? Here, from the cafeteria, take it. – No, we needn't share. – Don't mention it. My tucker bag is always deep enough for apples, postcards, hearing aids.

Don't think a person becomes a walker automatically, or by accident. Being brought up to go for walks begins early. At the age of twelve, at the latest, children used to walking can be identified as gentle, intuitive, brash, charming or serious walkers. – No, the apple's for you. I don't want half. – If that's how you *accept* something, Kâzim, I wouldn't like to see you trying to *give*.

Serious walkers need to complete the full length of their walk, to do that hard work. They want to *accomplish* something. Adversities – such as a wind tugging at them – permit them to feel a determined pleasure. Serious walkers often grow to become mountain climbers. Keeping to elaborate schedules, step by step, inch by inch, they push their way up with their excessively heavy backpacks, past shady livestock barns, overtaking people who, light-footed and rucksack-less, shout 'Hello' after them, to which the serious climbers reply, 'Morning!' No alpine pasture is too steep for them, no thicket too dense. Having reached the top, they drop onto a stone, in a spiritual pose.

– Charming walkers? When they smile, the whole world smiles with them. They *know* that, and like to smile a little too often and too much. Charming walkers can get away with those unflattering comments you'd never forgive someone else for. They turn everyone's heads. Only a few remain single. In the event of divorce, they're given the children.

How does a charming walker approach an attractive woman? He steps on her foot outside a clothes shop. The woman expresses her pain with an 'Ouch'.

The charming walker apologises. 'I'm terribly sorry, please forgive me. I'm not normally so clumsy. May I treat you to a cup of tea?'

Naturally, however, these strategies are subject to fashion.

My wife was an intuitive walker through and through. You can't imagine a more fraught activity than that of accompanying an intuitive walker. A thousand times, I regarded Emilie as a headless chicken. A walk for her went hither and thither: forward one moment, back the next. Straight paths didn't seem to exist for her. Where she was heading one minute was by no means an indication of where she wanted to be next. Once, Emilie went to get milk for our freshly roasted coffee, and came back with the farmer's wife and her three sisters-in-law. While doing the shopping, she regularly went walkabout, never to be seen again. And again and again, it turned out that, however absurd it might seem, she *did* find her way back to where her walk had begun, and had been right to turn off where, actually, she shouldn't have been right to, at all. She did whatever came to mind, and it wasn't advisable to try to talk her out of it. For this gentle, helpful person could then become a stubborn mule. If someone recommended we go for a walk through the Jewish Cemetery in Berlin, Emilie would thank the person enthusiastically for the good advice. Then we'd get off the train far sooner, in Kassel, because she'd recalled that, the previous evening, our three-year-old son had pointed to the unfolded map of Germany and enigmatically pronounced: 'different place!' She sometimes felt sorry for cyclists not being allowed to go backwards or sideways. As I see it, cyclists are always free to get off their velocipede and continue on foot.

Emilie was always doing something or other, or everything at once. Professionally, she wavered for a long time between tour guide and hotelier, then became a dressmaker and a housewife and looked after the neighbours' children and their children's children, who would frolic around and make a racket, which explained my moodiness at home. The whole place would be crawling with children: Markus on the pedal tractor, cheerfully shouting 'Fire! Fire!'; Roberto making a big fuss about looking for the red felt-tip pen; the others hopping around and squealing; and Emilie – cool as you please – carrying an infant on her hip, or asking, 'Could you hold the baby for a moment, Lukas?'

'Gladly,' I'd answer, obligingly, accepting the infant in as relaxed a manner as an American soldier handed an un-addressed parcel while on patrol at 40° longitude in Korea. Herr Probst! – You're certainly in a hurry! – The hot milk and bread? – No, I thought it was tasty. – No, certainly not. – Oh dear, oh dear! – Why, yes, that's what I'd do, too. – For sure. Tell the manager that until it's clarified whether the food contained poison, you'll refuse all forms of nourishment. – Don't mention it, Herr Probst, you're very welcome!

Are you intelligent enough to know that astrology is based on superstition, Kâzim? Emilie was intelligent enough not to take no notice of it nonetheless. Wasn't there something I wanted to ask Herr Probst?

You never know what will occur to Herr Probst next. Often he says something sensible, no *really*, but occasionally something completely hare-brained, too. Poison in the milk and bread. When he's about to start, it's always interesting to guess what he might come out with. Either way – sensible, or not – he has the same *spontaneous* air.

Herr Probst built up his own business, then had to hand it on. He'd not reckoned with the retirement age applying to him one day, too. His greatest wish is for the management to phone and say, 'Herr Probst, a revolt is taking place here. Regardless of what your pension plan states – please come out of retirement! Your firm needs you!'

Until such time as that call arrives, Herr Probst is keeping himself busy with other mysterious phone calls. He stares at the stone floor beneath the payphone in the entrance hall while, at the other end of the line, the dainty sales assistant of a mail-order company turns in her office chair and, distraught, summons, I imagine, her branch manager.

'Your company has sent me an axe I didn't order,' Herr Probst says, into the receiver. 'No, I can't simply send the item back. Because of the packaging. I've . . . – No, moreover, it's pretty heavy. I'd prefer it, young lady, if the company would simply collect it. – Probst, Meinrad Probst. Listen, you work for this mail-order company. You can tell the difference between things, I take it? You can imagine, no doubt, that an axe and a corkscrew are very different things? No? – Listen, I'm not exactly young any more, I've maybe only a few more bottles to uncork. Surely you don't want to be the reason the time I have left goes badly? Please connect me with your superior. Please connect me . . . – No. I just want to know how we can arrange for you to collect the axe, because if I send it by post . . . ' but yes, I know, Kâzim. I shouldn't need the stories of strangers, snippets from other lives, to give myself a boost.

A stairwell can't be designed generously enough, to my mind – how do you see it, Kâzim? A staircase has every right to be broad and bright. The removals men would like to be able to carry furniture up or down without first having to dismantle it. The emergency services would be pleased if residents could be *stretchered* down to the ambulance. Also, when they leave for the last time, residents should have the right to be carried down the stairwell. There were the chef, Lydia and I, waiting in the Breakfast Room with a cake and pastries to wish Herr and Frau Dürig another happy year of marriage, and yet Herr Dürig, tall and broad-shouldered even in his old age, had already been ferried out in the goods lift, like a damaged pedestal. Since the conversion, the 'adaptations', this staircase has been anything but generous, I have to say. Despite the paintings that change with the seasons. The Home's central location, the view from the attic and the pretty courtyard are really the only things that, for me, justify the hefty service charges. And the people – *of course*, the people – the old and the ancient.

Basically, I know nothing at all about most of my fellow residents. But it's impossible, even with the most secretive fellow resident, not to become aware of things that are none of one's business, for example the number of visits per month, or pointers regarding his health. Many a fellow resident shows no sign of any interest in the others living here, they try to avoid you, if at all possible, take care not to ask questions, are evasive if they themselves are asked any. But not even these spoilsports can get away with not saying 'Good morning' or avoid brief comments on the weather. Every human being demands attention from another, simply by virtue of being close by. I barely know most of the residents at all, but actually all of them interest me – some more than others, I admit, depending on their behaviour and my level of weariness – but they do all interest me.

Whether you wish to or not, Kâzim, at some point you'll begin to bother your head about the people among whom you've landed here. And the odd thing is: if you begin to take an interest in all these strange old people, it soon turns out that 'old people' do not exist, but only ever exceptions to the rule. You'll come across exceptions constantly, believe me.

You know, I used to be a teacher. First, below the hump of the Gurten, then in the Emmen Valley that is foggy enough to conceal two enemy armies from each other. Later, in a sleepy hamlet between Lake Thun and Lake Brienz. My parents, expecting a post-war crisis, were relieved to see me entering a profession thought of as crisis-proof. At the start of each school year, I began every Geography lesson with the question, 'What is the Earth?'

'A sphere' was the required answer. Therein lay all my wisdom. The earth is a sphere. Countless paths lead from person to person. School isn't about counting and spelling. It's about learning to get along with your fellow human beings. A great pity then that, in forty years, no one understood that. What did you learn at school, Kâzim? The seated way of life? To be punctual? Not to contradict, and to put up with being given marks?

I remember one lesson. I'm teaching as usual and the young people are seated before me, anything but mesmerised. Then I go for lunch. When I return, the pupils tell me, 'Marc was sent home.'

'By whom? How come?'

During the lesson, I had talked about how, in order really to get to know something, you have to experience it for yourself. I impressed upon them, 'If you want to know what a roof is, then you have to climb onto the roof, feel the tiles, sit on the crown and listen to the wind sweeping over it. Then you'll be able to say, I know this roof.'

Veronika answered, annoyed, 'You don't have to have been somewhere to know about it.'

Ever since I explained the meaning of school to her, she no longer trusted me.

After the bell for noon, the pupils told me, Marc had climbed onto the roof of the school. In the yard down below, dozens of pupils had gathered, shouted, waved, thrown chestnuts, but he wasn't to be deterred. Only when the care-taker had dragged out a long ladder and the head teacher, fearing for his life, had scaled the wobbly rungs, had Marc moved. He'd scrambled across the roof and vanished into a skylight.

So I go to the head teacher's office, where the latter doesn't exactly welcome me with open arms. 'So you come to this school and tell the children to climb onto the roof?' he rages. 'You're a danger to my pupils!' He doesn't let me get a word in. 'How dare you incite the children to climb onto the roof! As if they weren't undisciplined enough as it is!'

And he goes on to talk about the education system, its growing value in educational and social terms, the teacher's task of giving the pupils a good start in life, especially these days. 'Who do you think is picking up the tab for your antics, Herr Zbinden?'

A boy sat meditating on the school roof hardly troubled him less than a load of dynamite. I don't know whether that head's still alive today. If so, he's in his late nineties. In any case – my methods didn't convince him.

So I visit Marc at his parents' place. Good-humouredly, he says, 'I was able to observe the storks on the primary school roof and, do you know what, Herr Zbinden? One day, I'd like to find out why albatrosses migrate with the wind round the Antarctic.'

'The head teacher . . . '

'Don't worry, Herr Zbinden, I've learned when I can climb onto roofs and when I can't. I won't get it wrong in future.'

What do you remember about houses built on stilts, Kâzim? If you want to know something, do you take out your History folder from the school year in question and re-do the sheets? I loaded the pupils onto the train and we headed for the lakes. We spoke to fishermen who waded through the shallows, to house owners at Lake Biel. What does it mean to live by the water? Ideally, the pupils wrote down nothing at all. Instead, they came to associate a concept with encounters they'd had. You might object that that would be significantly more difficult in the case of other topics. Africa, for instance. Maybe we knew someone who had been there? We invited René Gardi to have coffee and cake with us, and he told us about riding across a barren desert, accompanied by two able natives who had fled from a bloodbath in Ghana and were now cheerfully awaiting his instructions.

Do you know what our biggest problem in life is? My daughter-in-law thinks it's the educational path her daughter will take. My son thinks it's the power steering on his petrol explosion engine. Frau Wyttenbach thinks it's Herr Hügli's tom, Herr Imhof that it's Herr Hügli when the latter spits half-chewed meat back onto his plate. Frau Felber thinks it's her second-hand kidney, Herr Furrer worries about his great-niece's happiness and the supposedly fantastic restaurant with a wood-fired oven, albeit in the most inhospitable valley of the Jura, that she's intent on running if he'll cover half the asking price. And you, Kâzim? Do you think, perhaps, it will be what to do when you've done your time here? – By then, you're sure to have quite different problems, believe me.

Listen: the biggest problem in our lives is the jadedness that can set in. Eyes, ears, nose: all dulled by constant stimuli. The world lacking all sparkle and clear contours, a dull grey, and foggy. No difference, whether it's day or night. The one thing that offers any brightness: relaxing as you brush your teeth with your carer, or longingly waiting for your family to visit at Easter.

As a teacher, I was always looking for new images to illustrate this jadedness for my pupils. I said, 'Imagine we were born with a thick fog in our heads. And every day we don't go for a walk, that fog thickens. We just sit where we are instead of going for that Sunday walk with our parents – a waft of mist. A day without making conscious use of our feet, our ears, our eyes – more fog. Consider how thick the fog must be, drifting in our heads. All those hazy impressions and sensations. The fog of jadedness.'

The image doesn't work, you think? My jaded-fog speech was directed at beastly girls and unruly grouchy troublemakers, but most of all at shy, disoriented, fast-growing teenagers, and whatever reservations you or I might have about weather conditions in our heads – I can assure you it made sense to the target audience in the way bright yellow lemonade does.

Didn't you ever get annoyed with teachers who promised some insight or other, only then to wangle their way out of it? They build weird apparatus, busy themselves with scales and a pendulum; table by table, they set up complicated experiments, but never do they explain what any of it has to do with our thoughts and feelings. In my day, whole herds of professors could survive comfortably in their chairs: all they had to do was acquire a highly polished desk with lots of secret drawers in order to concoct more new philosophical theorems, all in double Dutch. Now, I'm different. If I claim to have discovered some things, I don't go all coy and keep them under wraps just because they're simple. What use is it to anyone if I'm completely convinced I know better about something, but keep it to myself?

Are you a Sunday walker, Kâzim? That's those who go for a walk primarily because it's Sunday. They'd always be willing to forget the walk if there were an easier way of getting more fresh air and exercise, without exhaust fumes.

The centre of their lives lies beyond their walkable environment. The State endeavours to absorb the dissatisfaction of the Sunday walkers by reducing the number of places where they can walk.

It's best if I admit right away: walkers, to begin with, are as jaded as anyone else. But they can overcome that jadedness if they're prepared, afterwards, to devote some attention to their walks. They resolve to remember their walks, and become accustomed to talking to someone about their experiences every day. Of course! You can also write about the experiences. You think a written sentence is richer than the observation that preceded it?

Grandfather always advised my brother and me to keep a diary. In a diary you write down everything you do, he told us.

'Everything?' my brother asked.

'Of course,' Grandfather said. 'Then you just have to hide it.'

We didn't know why you had to hide a diary. Soon, we did. On Saturdays, Mother always put the milk money in the milk box. We took fifty *rappen* from it and bought two lined jotters. The milkman complained, but Mother – bright red in the face – insisted she'd left the exact amount out. A terrible quarrel. To my knowledge, there had never been a bloody incident in our part of town, but Matthäus and I had the feeling there was one in the air. In the end, she paid the difference, but from that moment on we got our milk from another milkman. – Pardon? – 321? That's up the stairs here. The next floor, along the corridor and round the corner to the left at the end of it. May I ask why you're going there? 321's empty at the moment. – No. Has been for weeks, everything's upside down in it. – You're visiting your great-aunt? What's your great-aunt's name? – Ah! Frau Rossi's in Room 231! – 231, that's right! Down the stairs, second floor, along the corridor, second door on the left. – 231, for sure. – Don't mention it. – Yes, yes. There are a lot of rooms here, no shortage of them. She'll be glad of your company, that's nice, you paying her a visit. – Same to you!

Do you know Frau Rossi, Kâzim? – How come you know Frau Jacobs and Herr Hügli already, but not Frau Rossi? – Slight build, shy? Check in your list of residents. Her mother frightened her to death as a child with the story of a girl who watched a thunderstorm from her window and when the lightning struck, a replica of her face remained on the glass forever. Frau Rossi never forgot the story, that's for sure. – No, Frau Rossi hasn't been able to see properly for years. Blind, nearly. A result of her diabetes. When the sun's shining, she can only see a blue strip beneath her eyelids. Terrible. When Lydia was taking her to the toilet once, Frau Rossi got caught on a table leg and fell and broke her forearm. She really should do exercises, but doesn't dare leave her wheelchair. Should, ought to! Believe me, many a time here, you long for nothing more than a faith healer.

•

The second floor, generally, is associated with trouble, concern and adversity. Misanthropist Wenk sits on the hard elbow chair out in the corridor, saying nothing. Expressionless eyes. I've seen dead trout with a friendlier twinkle. It's said that, in the whole world, only four watchmakers are in a position to appreciate what that man has accomplished in terms of craftsmanship, and he no longer speaks to three of them. I think he thought all his life that a human being is someone who accomplishes something, and that the value of a person can only be measured by the quality of that accomplishment. That seemed an elegant conviction until his hands went numb. Whilst Herr Kleiber – Herr 'Money-never-goes-stale' Kleiber – Room 233. Reported his trustee to the police alleging that his income is no longer even 25 per cent of what it used to be; and he wants the gymnastics assistant to be arrested. Stole his left trainer, he claims; the proof is in her locker. Hard work, that man.

I can give you some advice to keep you out of trouble here, Kâzim. First: never touch Herr Kleiber's things. Second: don't worry if you get the impression the residents aren't speaking to each other. In the Prayer Group and the Biography sessions, they're working on it. Third: take the time to accompany elderly walkers when they request it. Fourth: the number of people on first-name terms here can be counted on one hand. Can you remember all that? The woman who takes the Biography sessions disappears for twenty minutes in every hour. – To drink coffee and chat, in the Office, to the head of Admin.

And Frau Grundbacher from 229? – You don't know her? Plump as a Mother Superior – if ever you're in need of shade, she's the one to follow. Spends the whole day trying to corner people. Then does nothing but bleat at her victims. Illnesses and wrongdoers: she has a great memory for every imposition she's ever been subjected to. Only new arrivals and the completely unbiased ever join her. Can you imagine how Frau Rossi must feel, stuck between 229 and 233?

I'm at Frau Grundbacher's door one evening. I knock, she lets me in. She complains again about her stomach operation, undertaken by an incompetent anaesthetist. I could pass an exam on the subject of her stomach. A day-by-day calendar is hanging on her cupboard. I tear a page from the calendar, roll it into a ball and throw it into her wastepaper basket. Frau Grundbacher looks at me, beginning to question my right to be there.

'Frau Grundbacher, the day is over,' I say. 'You didn't ask for it but, no doubt, made the best of it. Now it's gone, let's look forward to the next one.'

But how can we combat this jadedness?

Once back home, the walker reviews the walk. Was the river flowing freely in the green shade of trees or was it sluggish beneath a stormy-grey sky? Did a block of rock glimmer in the sun or did it languish in the rain? Did a passer-by's face light up with a smile or had it a handkerchief tied round it? Reality was different every time; it changed from step to step. Once back home, the walker again smells the beginning-to-wither blossoms and enjoys the view out over blue valleys and white mountains. He enjoys looking back, just as, now comfortable in his armchair, he enjoys a glass of wine that, in the inn in the valley, in his rush to get home before black clouds and impending thunder caught up with him, he drank in one gulp.

Have you met Herr Imhof from Room 103 already? Gaunt face, lot of sharp edges, snowy-white hair, always boasting about the Thurgovian blood in his veins? Retired Major. He says, 'Herr Zbinden, you always talk about walking as if it were the one and only thing in life. That's being fanatical. Isn't what people do in their spare time completely irrelevant?'

You can see what he's trying to say, can't you? Go for a walk, make a phone call, collect toy soldiers, sleep all day Sunday, play the French horn, spin honey, watch satellite television, indulge in booze-ups, affairs – the main thing is you enjoy something or other and have a deep respect for what isn't actually visible. No doubt, you see it that way too, Kâzim? It would be fanatical to play off one pastime against another. You agree with Herr Imhof, don't you? You don't need to be shy with me. You have the advantage of youth on your side, and I'm just a fool who knows as much about these things as the man on the moon. Don't you feel like arguing with me? – Are you saying nothing because I've one foot in the grave? What aren't you saying, in order not to appear impudent?

I once tried to get Herr Imhof to go for a walk. I literally forced him to leave 103. His room has an excellent view onto Brunnadernstrasse. By night, it's flooded with lamplight. Herr Imhof reports sinister incidents. Lately, the police checked out his tip-off when he claimed a woman had been abducted in the late evening by a man in a delivery van. Turned out: the woman was paralysed, and the man a taxi driver.

'What's wrong with you young ones?' Herr Imhof shouts, leaning out of his window and staring, disgusted, at the young people balancing on their sports bikes on the pavement below, with one hand against the wall.

'Come with me into the courtyard, Herr Imhof,' I say, to cheer him up. 'The natural stone, the nettles – what am I saying? – the chestnut in bloom! Let's do a trip round the world right here.'

'Leave me alone, Zbinden. I've a terrible headache.'

'You'll have to vacate your room soon, in any case. Frau Beck wants to change the bed linen.'

Outside, an embittered Herr Imhof stares straight ahead, noticing neither the nettles at the fountain, nor the other residents. 'Bitch,' he mutters, through clenched teeth. 'Bitch! She wouldn't be able to take her life by persuading a snake to bite her. Faced with biting her, the snake would rather die.'

I don't know which affair with which woman is darkening his mood. Who can know another person's thoughts? You can only know as much about them as they wish to let you. Suddenly, he steps out, smartly, as if in the army, perkily and with dignity. He looks up and calls over, 'Hey, Zbinden! Why are these scientist guys always working at ways to prolong life, instead of finding an efficient way to end it? I've worked out whether throwing yourself from the window in the attic would be fatal. It would, for sure, but the roof conceals the view – and so you can't see where you'd land. Maybe in a flowerbed. Maybe on the caretaker's parking space. Goodness, Zbinden, don't look at me like that – as if I've gone crazy!'

He sits down on the stone bench at the fountain, contracts his muscles painfully, and sits there, motionless. I inform him that the fountain is exactly 264 paces from his room, three paces for each year of his life, but it doesn't seem to cheer him much. He just grunts.

Herr Imhof: a spent match. Up until a year ago, he always wanted to be first out of his room, and at the breakfast table by seven at the latest. There, he could say 'Good morning' to all the women, and compliment them.

'I dreamed of you last night, Barbara,' he might say, beaming, as the kitchen hand hurried past with freshly baked loaves. 'I heard your voice; you were singing a song. And I was following your voice, as if compelled to.'

He called the women queens, and if one of them had a delightful name – Julia, for example – you'd have thought he was going mad. Frau Jacobs comes in, he plucks at his lips and says with grief-stricken eyes, 'Julia! I've not seen you for two days. You don't love me! But I'll do anything to win you over! Caesar scented the sails of his ships to make Cleopatra desire him even from a great distance.'

Frau Jacobs retorts, passing, 'You're not in your right mind.'

Herr Kleiber, unsettled by a letter from his estate agent, turns to Herr Probst. 'The years haven't made Herr Imhof any wiser. He'd still prefer a woman over money.'

Herr Kleiber has asked for a price for his former home that he himself thought absurdly high. His estate agent is informing him of a buyer who accepts the price. Herr Kleiber immediately smells a rat: the price must be too low. He wants to take the house off the market, to try again in six months – at a higher price.

'What is money?' Herr Probst says, dreamily. 'All it takes is for a dry summer to come along and it all gets drunk away.'

Herr Kleiber shakes his head and turns to Herr Pfammatter, who is lost in thought. 'Love fades, but money never goes stale.'

Herr Pfammatter is silent, angry, because, a few minutes ago Hügli's tom badly scratched a priceless, incredibly valuable Glenn Miller record that, in his day, Herr Pfammatter had smuggled out of a music shop in Antwerp under his coat. It has touched him to the quick to see the record so badly scratched. He would have liked to take the tom by the tail and whack it round his four walls, but controlled himself and just threw it out of the room.

Once, the knife fell from Frau Jacobs' hand and bounced at Herr Imhof's feet. He bent down and returned it with a wink. Without even looking at him, she accepted it back with the words, 'I could've done that myself.'

'You really will have to learn to adjust, Frau Jacobs,' Herr Imhof replied with his barracks voice – menacing sentences, gradually gaining in volume – 'You'll still have to meet a requirement or two, if you wish to become Frau Imhof.'

For a few seconds Frau Jacobs looked at him, her interest suddenly flaring, as if she wanted to establish which planet Herr Imhof was living on. Then, melancholy and pensive, she looked into nowhere and said, 'It's not just that you don't always get what you want. Most of the time, you get something and don't begin to know what to do with it.'

Those were the final words the two of them ever exchanged. Repeatedly, I find myself hoping it might yet turn out to be a story with a touching ending. Lady Jacobs and Major Imhof, alone in the dark corridor on the third floor, both groping for the light switch.

Watch out, Kâzim. As soon as a new carer comes along, Herr Imhof mourns the passing of his predecessor, even though he was always dissatisfied with that one too.

The hours I spend, wandering round this city, unaccompanied. Even when they don't involve a special encounter, I like to remember them. May I tell you about my walk yesterday? – Before the memory pales? Hügli's tom dozing, its legs stretching out ominously from beneath the bench at the entrance. Lydia, running after me to give me an umbrella, though it's not raining. The hum of the caretaker's electric hedge-clippers. The cloud, the shape of Italy. Bobby, at the tram stop, looking for his multi-journey ticket in the inside pocket of his jacket. Dry leaves from last autumn, stubbornly clinging to the shrub. Cloud cover, looking like the Near East now. The nice cosy fire on the tarmacked car park beside the Art Gallery. Fingernails, cut short, carefully, and manicured red. The sparrows that venture out in the damp air. *Fuck performance* and *Be friendly to concrete* – new graffiti, scrawled overnight, in the urinal at the Zytglogge. The dying potted palm at the Kornhaus. The young woman who, while straightening the collar of her blouse, tweaks at her hair, turns her rings, and – in the narrow space between the hot dog counter and the drinks dispenser in the Migros Take Away in Marktgasse – acts out the minor tragedy she was involved in at her workplace. The coffee beaker that drops from a woman's hand and remains upside down on the pavement. The girl with the brace and her school stuff outside the jewellery shop, her gaze fixed on a sapphire. Chocolate gateaux and chocolate bears, vying for space in the window. That very specific kind of young, unflinching men, their beer bottles at the ready for throwing, who make me step up my pace, want to put some distance between us. The Iceland cloud, its shadow flitting over the wall of a house and my path: a lilac and some laurels fade, then light up, bright green. The property over in Obstberg on which, where before there were a few shrubs and a patch of brown grass, a swimming pool has been created in just a few weeks by some hardworking men from a construction company, who dug and staked out and removed sludge and huge great stones, their forgotten Marlboros hanging from their lips. Frail people like me, who – unlike me – aren't on the path along the Aare in the early mornings, preferring to relive their youth by watching a wartime pin-up on TV. The iced-tea teabags, the crumpled crisp bags and the still glowing butts of roll-ups that show a herd of tech college pupils passed a few minutes ago. Swarms of pigeons shooed into the air. The dark prints on the pavement, left by the leaves removed by the Highways Department. The umbrella stand, with the appropriate sticker on it, ready for the bulky refuse collection. The finger exercise audible from the window. The deaf woman at the market stall asking loudly for black bread, making it sound as if Heaven and Earth were passing away right then. The drizzle that proves children's playgrounds are played in even when there isn't any sun. Policemen, neither especially friendly nor polite, deliberately forgetting who pays their wages. On the fencing round a building site: shrill posters advertising a concert at the football stadium. Railway station guards, ensuring no one dares to sit on the stairs. The fire-, impact- and theft-proof payphones that permit you to have a conversation – postponed forever, it seems – with your own son. The orientation system for the blind that makes you think of nothing else for the rest of the day but Frau Rossi and your own eyesight and what good fortune it is to be able to see colours and faces, and always to know where exactly you are. How vulnerable everything is, and how easily something can happen. Don't sit on the banister, Kâzim, you could fall off.

I'm telling you about yesterday's walk, and I'll tell Lydia about it too when I return the umbrella, but understand: it's not the words that are important but the experience itself. I could continue for hours in this manner – and should any exciting adventure stories occur to me, I'll all too gladly tell you them. But a large part of what we experience drowns in words. Occasionally, I catch myself having the heretical thought that the time invested in telling someone about a walk might be better used going for more.

As a young walker, I liked to complement what I experienced with things I made up. An over-fed, milky-white dog followed me half the length of the canal.

'One of those nice little ones?' Emilie asked.

'A big, angry one. One that would grab himself a chicken, if some happened to cross his path.'

To entertain her more, I add a separation scene, and then a reunion. 'On the way back, the dog dropped a peacock feather at my feet' – and who knows what else.

But Emilie had a good feeling for which experiences were genuine and which made up. 'Is that all true, what you're telling me?' she might ask, pensively.

'Well, you shouldn't take it literally.'

'So it's lies. Quite simply, lies.' If I'd been a book, Emilie would have tossed me in the corner.

Her eyes were keener than a sparrowhawk's. 'Who broke the rose twig off?' she could ask.

I'd seen our son snapping it off, but why get him into trouble? So I explained it must've been a stray cat. The next day, Annemarie Gygax from across the way comes and shares with Emilie both who did it and that I observed the culprit. Or: the two bushes of ripe strawberries – why should I denounce the girls who had eaten the strawberries? I said I'd seen the birds eating them. I couldn't know that the girls' mothers would send them round to confess all.

'You lied to me, Lukas Zbinden,' Emilie said, angrily, and I stood there so exposed and ashamed, I could feel the weight of my shoes and the sweat in my armpits. Emilie had no time whatsoever for fibs.

And what did you do this morning that you'll soon have forgotten, Kâzim? Let me guess: washed and shaved Herr Mühletaler, together with Lydia; accompanied Frau Wyttenbach on her crutches to Gymnastics; talked Herr Kleiber out of the idea he'd been robbed? And at the weekend? – Really? Do you often go rowing? – No, I wouldn't be able. – You could be right. What I mean is, I can't imagine *me* doing it. – That's nice of you, Kâzim, but it's really not for me. I'd rather go home. By myself, if necessary.

While we're talking about walking: people who have had practice memorising their walks can soon report on lively experiences during them. They learn, for example, to tell one path from another. Can you tell one path from another, Kâzim?

Pavements, boulevards, promenades, arcades and tree-lined avenues; parks and gardens; gravel paths, pedestrian zones, elegant promenades for strolling along; sticky tarmac stretches, dusty country roads; beaten tracks, meandering cunningly; circular walks at altitude; entrances – full of pot-holes – to a farmyard ... There are paths that sing an eternally cheerful ode to the sun. Paths, weak and lacking confidence, that turn to the light and look for alms. There are devious paths that trip everyone up; tyrants that spread out at others' expense; hermits that have taken off all their jewellery and are doing penance. There are playful paths. Wise paths that have seen everything. Stout paths. Ponderous, dark, hate-filled paths. I can assure you, Kâzim: with time, paths reveal their essence to you. Flattered, walkers can see that all they have to do is help themselves. I don't know how you see it, Kâzim, but I find gently curving roads and paths that adapt to the natural terrain are preferable for the way they *steer* a walker. Motorways steer too quickly and too hazardously. Walking a motorway can feel arrow-like, a lethal walk.

My son always says, 'Walking experiences? I can tell you what you experience on a walk: annoying passers-by. Up the slope, down the slope. Accompanied by some kind of weather or other. Walking experiences? Experience of boredom, more like!'

I'd like to tell you something, as my son doesn't want to hear it: the art of not getting bored on walks lies in looking at the same object as yesterday, but thinking something different while you do. Have you noticed the nettles at the fountain outside? I look at them and think: they are green; being green is their great merit.

Do you know what I thought yesterday? Nettles can't fly. They are limited.

Markus, though – do you know what he's telling people? 'Only mad dogs and my father venture out in the midday heat.'

Saying that, the midday hour is the most pleasant for a walk. Oh, but yes. If the sun's directly above a walker, he needs nothing more than a sports cap to protect him from it.

In the late morning or late afternoon, there's no possibility of protecting yourself from direct exposure to the slanting rays. Which wrong theories do you have your relatives to thank for, Kâzim?

Wouldn't it be wonderful if we could share with one another the sensations triggered in us by the nettles beside the fountain, and gain an infinite number of images of those same nettles? Even the thought of such an exchange sends my heart thumping. My only regret is that my son doesn't wish to share that pleasure with me. What do you think, do nettles have any idea they exist? – Am I an old idiot? Markus treats me like one. But he has a screw loose himself. Do you know what he claims? 'Walkers always bring viruses into the house.'

Walkers bring viruses into the house? If there's an outbreak of influenza in every town and village, a disheartened walker will say: 'The day after tomorrow, at the latest, it will reach me too,' and become infected.

The undaunted walker walks among his sneezing and coughing fellow humans without coming out in sympathy with them. Markus drops comfortably onto the sofa, stuffs a few cushions behind his back, and looks at me condescendingly – as if someone who rears a walker like him hasn't the right to posit theories about disheartened and undaunted walkers.

Emilie was always undaunted. If rheumatic pains were torturing her so much that she had difficulty walking, she'd sit down in the armchair, rub Opodeldek into her knees, run her hand over the places that hurt and say, 'The pain's going away!'

Then she'd get up, do knee bends and order herself to set out into the countryside. Once back in the armchair, she'd be beaming, would massage her knees and ankles, and I'd have to tell myself I wasn't dreaming.

My weak legs. I count the steps to make sure they've not increased in number overnight.

Emilie's vitality was a mystery to me. One week she'd cart home-made soup along to those who needed it, and who would slurp and dip bread in it without a word; the next, she'd accompany the younger pupils to their ski camp and crochet doilies with the ones who had a cold or were injured. She was an active member of every organisation and charitable institution that existed down the years in our small town: Sewing Circle, Reading Group, leisure activities for the mentally handicapped, *Terre des Hommes*, her Woman's World group, the school board, the Summer Holidays initiative, she sang in two different choirs, her voice filled the whole room. She had three sisters and a brother; nineteen friends she'd known all her life; a hundred and sixty female colleagues she'd worked with at some point; and seven thousand acquaintances and relatives. You had to put on a fresh tablecloth, take out the good dishes and keep up to date about people who, in the fifties, were recovering from giving birth; in the sixties, forced themselves through marriages; only to abandon the same in the seventies, then go through 'phases' in the eighties.

You can't imagine my spiritual condition when obliged to participate in such socialising. Emilie would come up to me and try to tempt me away from my desk and down to the living room, where her guests were. I would raise my voice, 'No! I don't want to! I'll run away! How am I supposed to prepare young people for life with these constant disturbances?'

Emilie would wait calmly until I had cooled down and it wouldn't be long before she'd have me there at the tea table. They would talk about Martina, who'd stood behind Moritz and was now missing her 'own space'; about Herr Rechsteiner, a real gentleman who had presented the Woman's World group with flowers; about Tobias Wenger, who felt shattered, abandoned, misunderstood and inwardly all over the place. Vreni's doing the degree she didn't do before? And what about your Dora, does she like it in La-Chaux-de-Fonds? Marianne has decided in favour of Robert again; Franziska has a lover, married, a good-as-gold fool who feeds her sweets all day. Carlotta feels as if she's 'become invisible'; Annemarie feels 'out of things'; Frau Stettler is advised to try sage infusions to combat the unpleasant flushes; Frau Wehrli is fed up washing and ironing her husband's shirts; and Frau Schmidt starts talking about the old days when men still existed who spoiled you and cared for you and made you feel desirable. Years later, Frau Schmidt will remove the label from every single one of her husband's wine bottles before driving off on a motorbike, her arms around a stubble-jawed roofer. Almost all the married women complain that their husbands don't talk to them enough. Emilie points to Lukas

Zbinden who, throughout the entire conversation, has sat silently beside them, and says, 'He's the more talkative one in our relationship.'

The women blink, disbelievingly.

'It's true,' Emilie continues. 'He comes home and can't wait to tell me everything that's happened to him during the day, and what thoughts this fleeting day has sparked in him. For centuries, women were punished for talking too much or out of turn. They were tied to ducking stools and held under water till they almost drowned. Signs were hung round their necks and they were put in the pillory, they were gagged and tongue clamps were used to force them to be silent. In this household, my longest speech is always shorter than the shortest one given by my husband. The River Aare will stop flowing before his talk does.'

The women burst into laughter, and I am confused.

For weeks at a time, I completely ignored Emilie's social life, didn't take the trouble to ask who had come over to borrow onions, who she'd just been chatting with, singing with, collecting edible umbels with, to make fritters. An omelette batter, fried in hot fat. A delicacy sadly unknown to our chef here.

School holidays were something I dreaded. You never knew who Emilie would want to visit, never mind in which order we'd visit them. It became so complicated, we'd spend the autumn break apart. On the platform, I'd hug Emilie as though we'd never see each other ever again, and I'd literally shake my son's hand; he – despite my promise – would be rigid with fear that I might kiss him in front of strangers. I would travel with my teacher colleague Bertram to Weimar, or to the City of Equality and Fraternity where, through a bistro window, we could admire a Gallic city rain until such times as I sent Emilie a bouquet of flowers, or rushed into a phone box to tell her how very much I missed her. I'd walk through narrow Italian streets, looking sentimentally into other families' homes, enviously observing the afternoon *passeggiata* of moonstruck and less-than-moonstruck couples, and send Emilie wistful postcards that then remained for months in a strike-affected postbox in the railway station in Florence. In truth, I'd rather have travelled with Emilie, regardless of which of her sisters' homes I'd have imploded with rage in. I didn't want to be eaten up by missing her, but to travel with her and speak to her and look at her and touch her and hear her laugh.

If Emilie travelled somewhere on her own, she didn't cook in advance, nor did she leave notes telling the family how to cope. She simply set off on the agreed date. Without imagining the thousand terrible things that could happen at home in her absence. Full of enthusiasm, she'd get into the green carriage, sit down on the green bench and position her suitcase between her feet. Free of fear and cares – while, on the platform, I'd double-check numerous times that she wasn't about to go off in the wrong direction. I couldn't handle a whole week without her, but what I loved most about her was that she had a life of her own.

•

Emilie wasn't my first love, I have to admit. My incisors had yet to erupt when I pelted snowball after snowball at Margrit from the vegetable stalls on the Bundesplatz, and when I ran away, she ran after me and caught me, tore my knitted hat off and rubbed my face with slush. I didn't dare *speak* to Margrit, but I often pelted her with snow.

I was nine maybe when, for the second time, I fell in love with a girl not meant for me. Valentina was two classes above me at school and smelled of lavender. I admired her because her braids were so long she could sit on them. She was wearing a crystal-white dress, holding a fan and leaning against the firewood of the Residents' Association, stacked in its corrugated-iron shed. I can still remember my legs going and my carotid artery thumping so much my eyes blurred. I was throwing stones at the municipal trams, but Valentina just played with her fan and seemed not in the least interested in me. I held out the stamps I'd removed from a postcard from distant Portugal and hoarded like treasure in my trouser pocket. Valentina took them, only to proclaim, 'Romain ate an earthworm for me.'

That was the start of my misfortune. In the days that followed, I ate several handfuls of ants for Valentina, a number of butterflies, a small basket of cherries – she ate the reddish-black flesh, I swallowed the stones – a monstrous waste of ammunition for our catapults. On the terrace beside the Cathedral, she ran ahead of me, pointing her fan at a clump of grass here, a crumpled advert for bras and girdles from a fashion mag there, and I complied without a word. Without the slightest hint of admiration or even affection, she trotted off again, returning with a few woodlice or a spider that she proffered, wrapped in a cloth hankie. I'd barely finished when she pointed out, 'Romain ate three snails for me, the shells as well, and he only stopped because his mum called him in for tea.'

'May I kiss you?' I asked.

'Yes, but don't make my cheek wet, I don't like that.'

I may say that never again did I re-discover that smell of sweets, firewood and lavender on a woman's face. As you may well imagine, though, it was a good bit easier loving Emilie.

We waited for five years before we got married. I was guarding the Simplon Pass and, when there was a silver moon, could hear the melodic voices of the enemy. I played cards with my comrades, listened to Von Salis and his *World Chronicle* on Radio Beromünster and hoarded Emilie's letters. She, meanwhile, was mending army blouses and shared the concerns of the whole world at the time: emergency supplies, blackouts, rationing, problems with the heating, the possibility of evacuation. I'd sent her a handcart, just in case. Emilie presided over the Women's Association in Ostermundigen and organised a Sewing Circle, a Knitting Circle, a Christmas Parcel Circle, bazaars and clothes collections for the Red Cross. I wrote telling her I wanted to desert and come home and hide beneath the bed until the war was over. That was a crazy idea, Emilie wrote back, and she didn't want to hear any more about it.

Every free minute I had, I spent reading. I read her clever and soothing letters over and over till I knew them by heart. 'We look deep into the things that have become dear to us for the shine we ourselves project on them,' she wrote, adding a sentence by an unproblematic German philosopher who meant something to her. '*We see things not as they are, but as we are.* That said, we could just try being married, to see whether matrimony is annoying, or not. If it doesn't work, we'll proceed calmly and quietly towards a divorce. That way, no one gets hurt.'

I carried the letters around with me, in the inside and outer pockets of my uniform, and when the crumpled envelopes began to fall apart, I put the letters in a new envelope.

Then peace came along and, finally, the marriage became official. We accepted the keys to an apartment in Köniz, on the edge of Berne, went to the register office together, talked all night, listening to nonsense songs composed by Americans full of zest for life, then threw out our guests: Emilie's siblings who spoke six languages between them, yet talked in such a way you died of boredom while they were still on their mother tongue; our fathers and fathers-in-law who, from hour to hour, were agreeing more and more on how completely different all our war-ravaged neighbouring countries were – 'and they think *that* will all grow together into a single *Europe*?' Not forgetting our mothers and mothers-in-law and grandmothers – offended, even appalled, because they'd have preferred to see the bride in a white veil and to have organ music and a priest's blessing, preferably in the Cathedral.

Once the convivial part had broken up, I turned the glasses over on a cloth to dry and stepped into the bedroom and – you want to experience this one day too, Kâzim: Emilie was standing by the bed, in the altogether, nothing but a pearl necklace, and smiling at me, not entirely unselfconscious. Right there and then, her normally quiet, composed husband dropped the briefcase he'd received as a wedding present and chased her round the room.

Two mornings later, we found a postcard in our letterbox. 'Dear Tenants, You've now been in your new apartment for two days. We hope you've been settling in nicely. You've no doubt noticed by now that here on Fliederweg it's very easy to see into each other's apartments. Especially at night, if the lights are on and you've forgotten to close the shutters and the curtains aren't closed. Please bear in mind: current and future pupils of yours are watching. With kind regards, Your Neighbours.'

It's possible my debut as a teacher in Köniz wasn't a complete triumph. It's a wonder I didn't re-pack my things immediately when I saw the classroom I'd been given: a hovel, riddled with dirt and mouse-holes; bare bulbs hanging from the ceiling on long cords; on the wall, a rather flat relief map, Switzerland before the folding of the Alps. With my back to the militant class, I searched the sponge tray frantically for a usable piece of chalk. At the end of the lesson, the sweat was dripping from my brow and I'd banged the table so hard that the local clerk's son was beginning to worry about the furnishings. Have you seen this, though?

The pattern on the wallpaper here doesn't match the rest.
And there's a bulge in it here.

I'm in the habit of saying to my anaemic, pale-faced daughter-
in-law, 'Go for a walk before you start sniffing at the curtains
like an addict or using your tweezers to clean the logo on
the home stereo. Before you try to stay sane by indulging in
murderous fantasies while you hoover the tiger-fur covers
on the front seats in the car.'

Of course she wouldn't be able to go for splendid walks
right away, even if I did manage to persuade her. Senior
citizens who have practised all their lives can maybe go for
splendid walks – equipped with a sailor's cap, a tucker bag
with tassels and a beautiful stick on which they lean for
support, the right shoe badly worn at the heel. Without this
kind of practice, most people remain second- or third-class
walkers. Walkers who have only a loose – less than obser-
vant – contact with the world outside; walkers who don't
notice the sensations to which they are exposed. What is
sensational, after all, is that sensations don't appear to be
sensations. You step out of the door of a morning and find
the newspaper in the letterbox, and you remain completely
calm because the same thing happened yesterday and will
happen again tomorrow.

My daughter-in-law drops by: clattering heels; vampire-
blue, soon-to-be-fifty eyelids. She unpacks a pullover,
drowned-in-dye, for me; sinks crookedly into the armchair in the Day Room; asks whether the chair couldn't be

upholstered again; then gets onto her favourite topic of the moment: what will become of Angela if she actually passes her exams next year? I answer, truthfully, that I don't know. She removes her hand from her hair and stares at me in silence, devastated by the realisation that I can watch with such indifference as a family member hurtles towards misfortune. The handling of Verena's hair: something always seems to need doing on her head. Hair is constantly being caressed and put behind her ear; or ends are being tugged at; or all five fingers, even, work at the roots. Maybe she should risk a decelerated walk for once? What do you think, Kâzim? Maybe she'll *walk* to the shops for once? My daughter-in-law says she's constantly exhausted and cold, and I tell her what she can do to stop that. Is that not permitted? People only ever do what they want, I've understood that much. I know that no one ever accepts advice.

Verena takes a tablet while I'm at the window, looking out. I turn round and she's just closing the blue-and-white tin. 'On holiday,' she claims, 'in attractive places – there, I do go for walks. Until I drop.'

It's just that walking time can't be accumulated. You can't catch up on walks you didn't take. Walk for five hours and you'll feel worse than after three hours. Walks that last longer than an hour and a half, two hours at best, offer no additional gain.

Emilie always refused to accept that. 'I know my body,' she would assert. 'And I know it does me good to walk for five hours if, for several days before, I've walked just a little or not at all. I feel better afterwards.'

On nocturnal walks, Emilie was often the last decent soul to head past the darkly populated Golden Anchor, in the direction of Rugen. For a nocturnal walk of several hours along the River Lütschine, she'd pack a torch and replacement batteries, a whistle and a compass, some pulp fiction – protection against the cold – and a warm drink in a flask. Motionless, I would ferment among the forest's excretions while, by torchlight and in a croaky voice, Emilie read me a gruesome ghost story. She could identify the outlines of little birds in the shade of a thicket where, even after she'd shown me the exact spot, I could only see a black wall of leaves. After experiencing the different types of darkness, the adventure of the starry night, and ghostly figures and bat-wings rushing towards us, we returned home, chilled to the bone. We struggled to open the leather buttons on our coats with numb fingers. How can we look attractive when we screw our faces up so much they appear to be saying, 'Wasn't that unbearable?' Why don't we try to relax our features and think, as we do, 'What a wonderful cold night'?

Although, shortly after Verena's visit, my granddaughter looks in and walks round the Home with me. On the day she was born, I immediately opened a savings account for her, for her education one day. Such were the overwhelming feelings of happiness I experienced, I couldn't think what to do for her. Now she's a tall young lady, by far the prettiest in the family – like her paternal grandmother, more than anyone else. Even if less bashful than her grandmother, she beams with joy as she tells me how she persuaded a teacher at the grammar to let her off some homework by hinting she'd period pains.

The girls in my classes, in the past, never mentioned menstruation to me; not ever. I don't know what was behind that; a woman should be proud of her monthly cycle. It's fantastic what goes on in a female body: the womb, what the ovaries do . . . If ever I started on about it, Emilie would change the subject.

The smell of the pullover Verena gave me makes me feel sick. I put my head back and breathe through my mouth, but the feeling of nausea won't go away. I explain to my grand-daughter, gently, what the advantages and disadvantages of studying this or that are. Has she made a decision already? Maybe she just needs a bit more time to find out who she is and where her path is leading?

Angela blinks at me, mischievously. 'Granda, look at me properly!'

'You've ruined your eyebrows by plucking them.'

'Really nice of you to say that.'

'Out with it, then!'

'It's like this, Granda: I'm in love!'

'And I'm supposed to be able to *see* that?'

'Of course. The red cheeks, the glazed look . . . ' She gives a little laugh.

'Do you remember, dear Grandchild,' I say, 'it's not even three weeks since you told me – should you ever think of falling in love again, ever in your life – to box your ears, left and right, and if that didn't help, you authorised me to seek medical help for you.'

'Gabor was a monster.'

'I thought you'd established: all men are monsters.'

'Louis is an exception.'

'And who's Louis?'

'An exchange pupil. Twenty, and an excellent beach volleyball player. The way things are looking, we'll be using the money in my education account to start up a party-boat hire company – that also provides catering – in Marseille.'

'Generally, one thinks long and hard before taking the decision to start up a something-or-other that also provides something-else.'

She scrapes her pointy-toed shoes on the stones along the edge of the herb borders. 'Will you tell my fossilised parents, or do I have to do it myself?'

I imagine Angela going back to her parental home and dropping the bomb. A house with an English-style lawn and a decorated Hollywood swing, Markus swinging in it, looking at the broken guttering. Complaining to Verena that the mortgage has left him no room for manoeuvre, and that his white wine spritzer is too warm.

'I'm not going to uni,' Angela says, and her parents' eyes turn to her.

Verena slams her hands against her forehead, runs her fingers through her hair and pulls a terrible face. 'May I ask why not?'

'I need time to find out who I am and where my path is leading,' Angela explains. 'In the first instance, it's leading to Marseille. I'm trying out my independence. I take it you'll both want to support me in that?'

'We can gladly discuss it,' says Markus. 'But the whole thing, no doubt, has a lot to do with your grandfather, am I right?'

Angela stomps into the house, Verena swallows a sedative pill – or one to pep her up so the sedatives don't over-sedate her.

Believe me, if you've been married for fifty years, it's sometimes confusing to walk with someone else. Should you accompany me, Kâzim, I'll take care not to call you 'Dearest' suddenly or, with customary affection, to put my hand round your hips. Even now, my hand still reaches over mechanically to Emilie's side of the bed. What is a pullover like that made of, anyway? For sure, no material that comes from the back of an animal.

Of course, walking can be a form of torture. In the most civilised network of footpaths, there are sections even a well-established walker will find uncomfortable. Paths and pavements with baffling bumps, puddles, root damage, paving stones so far apart you get stuck in the gaps in between – that's how carelessly Highways Departments work. The use of pavements for purposes such as parking bicycles, public conveniences for dogs or storing road signs restricts our space. But things that are difficult, truly enriching, can never be fully appreciated if consumed quickly. Bach's organ pieces, Shakespeare's plays, the secrets of Space and of the ceiling in the Sistine Chapel: these all demand enduring and affectionate attention. It's no different when you walk tricky sections of a path. We decide what we may be subjected to. In time, we can feel at ease even on poorly maintained pavements.

For the sake of walking, you know, I took on some difficult country walks. For the sake of town walks, I had to accept fines. Yet if I had a hundred lives, from the first moment I could think, I would still become a walker. Regardless of how I earn my money, whether as a teacher again, or working at a planing, drilling or milling machine, as a moody house-husband, ant researcher, hereditary nobility or a street sweeper in an orange uniform – my life becomes meaningful the moment I go for a walk. – The fines? For stepping on private property, using public property without permission, causing an assembly of people that hindered traffic. Laws are made to protect us, but it's impossible for a walker to respect all of them. The assembly of people that hindered the traffic was caused when I gave a lecture to the young people at the Autonomous Centre, up at the bulwark, on the art of walking.

'Does this scene seem familiar to you?' I asked. 'You all sit down on a park bench in the Rose Garden and the elderly lady beside you clings to her bag especially tightly. Maybe your black clothes, heavy jewellery, your spiky dog-collar, disturb her? Explain to the lady her fear isn't justified. Offer to accompany her on a walk, and tell her about your deaf and blind grandfathers, whom you took for walks in the past but would never have used to beg for charity.'

Believe it or not, the young people crowded round me, amused.

Walking isn't taught at schools and universities; not a single one. No one seems to be interested in turning others into independent walkers, the type to think about themselves and their environment. Only those who don't know where they're coming from, where they're going, or what can happen in between, are glad to be the victims of all those who would chase them around. After twenty-five years of service, an underpaid, fully qualified cleaner is presented before the assembled staff with a bouquet of flowers, a certificate charred at the edges and a terrifying pin for her lapel. You're laughing, Kâzim. Is life a stage play, in your eyes, at which people laugh? Aren't you bang in the middle of it?

Where do you come from, Kâzim? – And your parents? – No, never, sadly. And my knowledge of Turkish is limited to a single expression: *Yavash soilarseniz daha eeyee ahnlahyah-jahyim.* – What that means? *Yavash soilarseniz daha . . .* – Don't you understand? No? Maybe you speak Turkish with a different accent? – Would it ever have occurred to you to appear before your teacher with a cackling goose under your arm, or a bottle of schnapps? That would be outright bribery, wouldn't it? – You can't begin to imagine the things Emilie and I experienced.

My second job. In the Emmen Valley, hellish for fog. We two the only heathens among nothing but holy joes who, completely serious, told me at parents' evenings that their son Ueli had decided not to sin, sin had ceased to exist for him after he'd fallen out of Eichenberger's cherry tree, and I should endeavour to encourage Ueli in his bid to please God. Emilie's contribution to the wall tapestry project on 'Creation' – Little Eve looking in the cupboard and beneath the bed and explaining via a speech bubble to Little Adam that she's looking for God – is rejected by the parish council as 'too free-thinking'.

A few weeks after I take up my post, a tractor stops outside and Ueli's father unloads two very full sacks. I look at Emilie to check, but she has ordered neither a sack of onions nor 100 kilos of potatoes. The farmer says it's right enough and – by the way – Ueli's unhappy with his role as Judas in the Nativity play. I say: either we pay for this produce from his fields or he can load it back on his tractor. Ueli's father takes the money and begins to move off, confused. What kind of new teacher is this? When I accompany him to the tractor, I see a curtain moving in the house opposite. So that evening, I head out and announce that we paid for the potatoes and onions. *Paid!* The landlord's wife understands and nods, pulls a beer and pours me an elder schnapps. Isn't it okay to treat her Vreni's teacher to a schnapps? And what's what Vreni wrote in her Religion jotter supposed to mean? 'Corn is a deity!' Every few days, the girls in my class turned up before Emilie with bunches of flowers they'd picked themselves, beaming and hoping I'd now appreciate their best writing. At Christmas, the girls made coasters, little pots for chives and salt-dough models for Emilie, and the boys presented me with soaps and apple wine. We sent everything the parents donated back – apart from the freshly slaughtered rabbit a farmer gave me as a birthday present. It wasn't that I wished to keep the rabbit, no, but we couldn't send it back because it had vanished without trace. Where was it? A pupil – Maria? Michaela? – snitched. It was Ruedi, the donor's son. Ruedi had got really angry because he couldn't stand me, he'd removed the rabbit from the staff room, taken it home again, and said, 'As if I'm going to let that scoundrel eat our Fridolin!'

At the end of his time at school, I put my hand on Ruedi's now-useless cowhide school bag and acknowledged, 'You've got something. You'll go far.'

At some point, on a Personal Development course for teachers, I heard that, one day in Konolfingen, Ruedi had stepped up to the bench of his locksmith foreman with a carbine. I assume Ruedi then gained an insight into the workings of state authorities, something surely granted to very few.

How cold the winters were in the Emmen Valley! Ice covered the streams, the fields were rock-hard. Boys planning to fight in the yard were forced indoors by the biting cold. The teachers in the staff room were wrapped up in woollen jackets, coats and army blankets. A layer of ice formed on my coffee and the flame froze in the hearth. You could touch the flame. We broke pieces off and put them in our mouths. They tasted like *peperoncini*. In this inhospitable valley, our son was born, to the unbridled joy of the girls in my class, too. They sent little notes to the hospital in Langnau. 'Did it go well, Frau Zbinden? What does he weigh? Is everything about him in proper and working order? Our teacher has such a happy cough.'

I had been born and grown up in town and didn't ever feel quite at ease out in the country, though I taught in the Emmen Valley for more than fifteen years. For a town walker, this region was as little capable of being a permanent residence as Elba was for Napoleon. In the sixties, I switched to another school, and we moved to a miniature town between Lake Thun and Lake Brienz. Power plant, tourists for the skiing, Italian restaurants, two pharmacies, a double gym hall and two thousand households. Close by: sunny mountains and trees and shrubs and protected shoreline for Emilie's country walks.

We rented a house not far from the Aare and focused on fitting in. A lightweight house, such as children often draw: a door in the middle, two windows downstairs, two windows crouching beneath the gable roof. Rose bushes on both sides of the door, seasonal joys in the garden. The walls became multi-coloured; a washing machine and oil-fired heating were installed; a Bernina sewing machine acquired; Emilie's workshop kitted out. 'Frau Zbinden, a seam has burst on my blue dress. Could you . . . ?'

The women of Lower Goldey – as far down as Seidenfadenstrasse – proclaimed their delight when they fetched the altered garments from Emilie, and those who were especially thrilled got a discount. Emilie knew about cutting to size and sewing, she'd come in with a tape measure in her hand and walk around you twice and before you knew what was happening, you were taking a seat beside your spouse in the chandelier room in the Victoria-Jungfrau in a dress that left the Dutch and English ladies at the neighbouring tables speechless.

'Is there a problem?' Emilie asks when Annemarie Gygax throws the fourteenth dress over the folding screen.

'It's pointless,' Annemarie sighs. 'Nothing suits me. Really, nothing at all.'

'This is what to do,' Emilie replies. 'Ask yourself, what do I want to say with this dress?' She lifts one garment after another from the floor and holds it up against Annemarie. 'Do you want to say: hi, look at me, the pearl of the evening? Do you want to say: quiet, inconspicuous, but deep within is a horse thief trying to get out? Do you want to say: I'd a rotten week, so let's drink the wine before it turns? Or do you want to say: I'm here with my husband but open to offers?'

'I want to say: I had to put the children to bed before I left, and to write the phone numbers down for the babysitter in an emergency, and hope you didn't all wait for me to arrive before you started the first course.'

'Good, kitchen apron and feather duster then,' – and I would leave our enchanted house. It took me about twenty minutes to reach my desk at the school, but going home often took longer for, along the way, there were many opportunities for gentle escapades: the crossing known as 'Robbers' Corner'; the benches on the square outside the town hall, where I could warm my stomach and look forward to Emilie. Once I witnessed a biblical-style Flood from there. An inky-black sky, then the sluices opened above the town. In a matter of minutes, the street had become a river, the women pulled their skirts up and, knee-high in water, fled into the bakery or gave each other piggybacks across the bridge to Interlaken that saved them. – You don't believe me? Emilie was piling sandbags against the garden fence as I approached, dripping wet, in no hurry, but with a certain feeling of security, as with a firmly secured property.

If people moved in, Emilie paid them a visit. Alone, or heading a small reception committee. She took presents to welcome them, a basket with bread and salt, a bottle of mineral water, and introduced herself to the new neighbours. Emilie was so full of beautiful things she could share with others. Her whole life was sharing with others, just as I wish that for my own life. Believe me when I say that, it's why I'm working at becoming inwardly rich. So that every time I'm together with someone, I can share something with that person.

I remember a walk at Lake Brienz. Sand, pebbles, upturned boats. Our two-year-old son ran to the lakeside. I spotted this and wanted to stop him. Emilie held me back saying, 'Let him run!'

And the little chap – he could hardly stay upright – continued to wobble down the slope. The story has a happy ending: my son didn't drown.

You see, Kâzim, on the first floor it's dark even if the sun's shining outside, and everything's wrapped in a deep silence. Back there, that's Herr Wenk. He's not half fierce, eh? Go on, give him a friendly wave.

Why I liked Emilie isn't hard to understand. But I often ask myself what she got out of me. For years, I had the uncomfortable feeling that I owed her something. From all the things I boast about having never learned – shopping so as to have things in reserve, replacing shampoo and suntan lotion, tying up the papers for recycling, answering the phone, writing thank-you letters, watering the flowers, raking the garden paths, killing off the weeds, storing left-over food in freezer bags – you can easily deduce what Emilie spent her time in the house doing. For her, gardening was a pure joy – was seeing things grow. For me, it was a sore back.

If I lit a fire in the nature reserve, she might come running across the picnic area and throw her arms round me. 'What a wonderful fire you've got going!'

And I'm thinking: Oh God, I need a dozen copies of the *Volksblatt* and a mountain of tinder-dry chippings, and I'm creating so much smoke, the animals are fleeing in droves from the forest. Sooner or later, she'll find out the truth and despise me. What does she see in me?

I know my physical appearance is okay. There were years when I actually looked attractive. But it didn't matter how good I looked, for as soon as Emilie stood in front of me, I was convinced she could see right through me to the scrawny, clumsy boy who, when the cadets were playing, hid with his piccolo behind his big brother, afraid of being eaten alive over a few wrong notes.

'Emilie, what do you see in me?' I could ask her, and she'd sit down on the sofa, stroke my arm and answer, 'Lukas Zbinden, you are endearing just the way you are. You think you need to be something more, but you don't. You are a Scorpio, and scorpions, characteristically, can bend their tails over their own back, ready to sting themselves. Bid goodbye to an old friend: self-criticism.'

How do you measure intelligence, Kâzim? Right at the top of the official list is the ability to figure out complex problems very quickly, to be able to read and write at a certain level, and to solve algebraic equations in a flash. Emilie considered the ability to enjoy every single day, and every hour of every day, a more reliable gauge of intelligence. The happier you can make yourself, the more intelligent you are. For children, it's natural to find yourself beautiful and see yourself as terribly important, but later you internalise the demands made of you by your environment. You weren't put on this earth to like yourself, that's not the point – what are others to think of you, in that case?

'Face the fact,' Emilie said. 'The person with whom you spend most time in life, is you yourself. Learn to like yourself.' She pressed my arm gently, and my muscles tensed involuntarily. 'Lukas Zbinden, I didn't know you have a bicep!'

So I stuck a post-it on the bathroom mirror with the prompt: 'Like yourself!'

My self-doubts didn't lessen. I put another post-it on the mirror: 'Like yourself anyhow.'

That helped.

Frau Grundbacher, a very good d – Pardon? What jumped out? – There, there. You have to be more caref– Of course, prevention is better than suffering later. – Well, no. – Oh, it's outrageous, all the things you can learn from day-by-day calendars. – Kâzim is right, that's a nice Zimmer-frame you have there, Frau Grundbacher. New, is it? – No, it is, it is, a nice colour – as Kâzim says – very plain. You haven't met? – He's our new carer. Has latched onto me and engaged me, against my will, in conversation. – Well then, Frau Grundbacher, let's look forward to tomorrow. – Goodbye. – Here, Kâzim, round the corner, let's attack the next floor.

You didn't half butter Frau Grundbacher up! About to start moaning, she was, and you took the wind from her sails. Nice Zimmer-frame, you don't say! Isn't it amazing that we keep running into one another, Frau Grundbacher and I? I peep round every corner to avoid meeting her, and she goes out of her way to avoid me. Seems to be on good form, though. I shan't speak ill of her ever again. I'll try not to, believe me. On the other hand, conduct a survey. It will confirm for you that, after an hour in the vicinity of Frau Grundbacher, every rational person has the feeling that that was enough for the time being.

This morning, in the overheated Day Room. The rays of the morning sun coming in, making the yellow curtains glow. I write a wish down on a sheet of paper, a wish for the Worries box in the Dining Room: 'Fritters, please. Edible umbels.' Herr Ziegler is reading, with his reading-glass, *To the Roman Age in an Elevator*, a tattered archaeological excavation report, keeping up his fascination with adventures of the spade. Herr Feuz is filling out a competition card, to win kitchen cupboards to the value of five thousand francs, and is keeping the seat at the window for ninety-five-year-old Herr Eggenschwiler. Frau Rossi is sitting silently, motionless and trustingly in the wheelchair. A fly lands, undisturbed, on her hand. Herr Probst is telling Frau Dürig about his latest contact with the Customer Service Team of a mail-order company specialising in tools, while Frau Dürig sucks the remainder of the sugar from her empty teacup, teabag string dangling. Frau Grundbacher is explaining to a pitiful Herr Eggenschwiler, who isn't getting any closer to the seat being kept for him by Herr Feuz, what is going on in her stomach. This is the Home's contribution to world affairs today.

Sitting at the table next to me are Herr Hügli and Frau Lüscher-Stucki. The barely seventy-year-old Frau Lüscher-Stucki who, a few months after her husband's funeral, grew sick of eating alone at mealtimes. Occasionally, she toddles into the Dining Room in a ruby evening dress, still trying to straighten the collar, the clatter of trolleys and trays all around her. You'll soon see who I mean. White hair, tinted blue.

Herr Hügli moves his knight diagonally across the board. Frau Lüscher-Stucki gives a start. 'Just a moment!' she shouts, her shrill voice piercing the quiet of the Day Room. 'That's not what you do with the knight!'

Herr Hügli replies, 'Don't be such a nit-picker, Frau Lüscher-Stucki. The main thing is: we have fun.'

'Don't! Stop it!'

'You sound like a guinea pig,' Herr Ziegler butts in. 'Alessandra, could you stuff a cloth in Frau Lüscher's mouth, please? If everyone here were to scream like that, the doors and windows would rattle.'

'No!' Frau Lüscher-Stucki shouts, bravely. 'The main thing is: you play right!'

And – I can't stress it often enough – that's how it is with a leisure activity. What counts isn't that we have any old activity. Recently, a sad figure on the second floor said to me, 'I'm starving my way out of the world.'

What counts is that you have the *right* leisure activity. An activity with which you can live when it gets very dark; that gives you support in the face of major challenges; for which there are no requirements in terms of age and ability; that requires no proof of an unimpaired ability to think; an activity during which you can die peacefully. The opportunity to die peacefully as you do it is a great measure of the right-ness of such an activity. My grandmother continued going for walks, even at a fine old age. At ninety-four, she bent down so far to see a field flower, her heart failed.

Here in the Home, there are people who don't go for walks because they take exception to me. Before me is a young woman who explains, 'I'm doing work experience; I'm studying Psychology.'

I say, 'Nice. And what's new?'

What was her name again? Perhaps you know her

name? – Plaits, up, not down, work experience? Expression on her face like in a fashion catalogue? No? – She smiles, 'Herr Zbinden, I listened to you a little in the Dining Room before. You know, walkers aren't any better than other people.'

And off she goes. I get told stories about people like me: 'self-appointed life coaches'. One betrayed trust. Another took off with all the money. Things have happened all over with 'self-appointed life coaches'. What are you supposed to say in reply? No walker ever says: Follow me and be blessed. They say: Follow the path and be blessed. A walker who talks about walking like me is a signpost. With a signpost, it's not a problem if it's crooked, askew, or has faded in the rain. If you can see where it's pointing, at least. 'Do you want to avoid the walk just because you don't get on with the babbling idiot in your care home?' I say to . . . what-was-her-name-again?

Frau Lüscher-Stucki used to play in the Chess Club. Herr Hügli will have to buy a book on chess and practise in secret. He's not a good sport at all. Last night, he threw his cards down during the very first game and said, 'You can't expect me to play with these cards!'

I gathered up all the cards that had been dealt and noted down 257 points for Herr Probst and me. I'm ruthless in that respect. We knew right away there was something very wrong with Herr Otzenberger when Herr Hügli managed to checkmate him back in the Spring.

•

In the Dining Room, Herr Hügli puts well-chewed meat back on his plate, to feed to his tom later. A black-and-white tom that, with its patchy fur and the mysterious kink in its tail, looks a bit the worse for wear. Once a notorious street-fighter, now retired. *Of course*, it bothers people. Not half! Hügli's tom bothers everyone who thinks having cats in a home for the elderly isn't exactly hygienic. Cats aren't *always* dozing, after all. They climb, too, for example via the chestnut tree in the courtyard up to Frau Wyttenbach's room, where they crawl into her bed. Frau Wyttenbach, red-eyed and with a runny nose, complained to the management. The air here is full of cat hair, she said. You find it in your soup, up your nose, and the cushions in the Day Room have been torn to shreds, like someone's been trying out their claws on them. She demanded sanctions. As far as I heard, the manager promised Frau Wyttenbach to investigate if she submitted a written report that would then be discussed at a meeting. And with that, for him, it was kicked into the long grass.

Not for Frau Wyttenbach, however. What does she do? Quick as a flash, she whizzes across the entrance hall to the cellar door, where I've just seen Hügli's tom go down the steps. With a less than subtle kick, she slams the door shut, takes a deep breath, turns the key – then looks to see if anyone's seen her.

'Now, listen here, dear Frau Wyttenbach,' I say, 'that's not acceptable. It's cold down in the cellar. It may well be you can't stand Gandhi. But as I see it, everyone else likes him, and if you hurt him, they could come and take you away.'

A contrite Frau Wyttenbach opens the cellar door and throws Gandhi – who bolts to freedom as if he'd been trapped in the lift for days with an activation therapist – a treat. That's life for you. You invent non-violent resistance and liberate India, and five decades later, Herr Hügli names a dodgy cat after you.

On the other hand, a walker who fails to cope with a staircase is only a semi-expert in his field. We are, Kâzim, aren't we – aren't we going to complete this steep slope together? Posterity mustn't be able to say of Lukas Zbinden that his footwork was sloppy. And maybe then you'll accompany me outside? Feel free not to rush your decision, I don't mean to push you. But a walk would be a good opportunity for us to have a proper conversation, you and I.

What would you give a nineteen-year-old girl who already has everything? – It's to be a surprise. – I just thought you'd know, maybe. As a little girl, Angela loved to walk with her grandparents and parents along the River Lombach to the pier at Neuhaus on Lake Thun. She'd call out the names of the flora she saw at the edge of the path, my son called out the names of the cars passing, then they'd both complain bitterly to each other that the other didn't listen. On the way home, she'd pick golden-yellow coltsfoot from the edge of the ditch, or she'd sit down in the clay furrow at the golf course, which seemed a bit too energetic to her mother behind the camera. Emilie and I treasured the fact that always, when our granddaughter was around, much more happened than when we were alone. Often, we found ourselves back at the age at which children ask questions – when we'd ask twenty-nine questions in ten minutes. Which butterfly is that? What lives in a puddle, stream or pond? And anyway, are the stars in the sky just painted onto a curtain, maybe? We'd lift sticks from the ground and rattle them along wooden fence-posts.

On one occasion, my barefoot granddaughter, Emilie and I are listening to a song thrush that, just a few steps from our well-trodden path, is perched unusually low in a tree. It is so far down, a taller man could have grabbed it. A woman and a boy from the campsite pass by. The child hears the bird, pulls at his mother's hand and wants to stop. 'Look!'

The boy asks what the bird's name is, and the woman answers, 'Lark, now come on.'

To which Angela, genuinely astonished, responds, 'But, Grandma, it's a song thrush, isn't it?'

The bird is perched before us, and lit by the sun behind us. On its bright breast, every single browny-black fleck is visible. When it sings, we can look inside its beak.

'Let's see if it always sings the same melody,' Emilie says.

It doesn't.

'How does it manage to hold onto the branch? It's remarkable that the thrush can sit still for so long. I reckon it can sit longer on that thin branch than we can stand here, on firm ground. Shall we see which of the four of us lasts the longest?'

Angela and I want to. The bird's keen, too, clearly. We stand there for over fifteen minutes. Angela seesaws, spreads her toes, bends her knees. She pleads with the bird to sing *Ramseiers*, and it produces something that, with a *lot* of imagination, resembles that tune. In the same way as sometimes, at night, you think the wind is saying something. You see, Angela was an impeccable walker. And now – what do you make of this, Kâzim? The day before yesterday, she says, 'Grandfather, you're no doubt right: I need to cultivate the walker within me. One day, I'll . . . '

'One day?'

'Well, later.'

'Why not today?'

Angela makes hot chocolate for us and, pouring it from cup to cup, makes it go cold again. 'I'd like to, of course. And at some point, I'll do without all kinds of things to achieve that. But, first, we'd like to achieve something in life, Louis and I. And stop trying to fatten me up. I saw you pouring cream into the milk, thinking I wouldn't notice.'

I realise, though, distressingly, that my charming nine-teen-year-old granddaughter is determined to start moving up the tax brackets.

'Louis says Marseille's a fairy-tale town that will give you everything you want – as long as you're strong and brave enough to ask for it.'

'Perish the thought!'

Every single day, my grandmother took a walk through Schüpfen and had time to chat to everyone she knew. And imagine: back then, there were no washing machines and no Moulinex appliances. She had four children to look after, wooden floors that had to be swept, paraffin lamps, a wooden kettle. She scrubbed clothes with soap until her nails were bleeding. In winter, she had to get up at five to put a bundle of wood in the tiled stove so the schoolroom was heated by the time Grandfather and his pupils arrived. She'd time, though, to walk through the village every day. Does my granddaughter? No, she doesn't. Why doesn't she make the time? I think – in the background – there's someone badgering her. Someone who, like the lion tamer at the circus, is constantly cracking his whip and rushing people. I call this lion tamer *competition*. I take it you have an imagination, Kâzim? Competition takes us up a very high mountain, from which you can see far. It opens the curtains and we can see all the riches of the world and all its splendour. Competition says to us: I'll give you all of that, if you're industrious enough and compete well. Why should Angela sacrifice her youth to achieve prosperity, and then use up that prosperity trying to stay young?

'Have you heard about Ecuador's relaxed approach to everything? I've no idea how you calculate this type of thing, but according to official sources, the country's legendary sluggishness saves it seven hundred million dollars per year in healthcare costs. Even the President always turns up late for his English lessons.'

'Put any idea of me becoming a teacher out of your head, Granda,' Angela replies. 'Party-catering is a great job. And don't say, yet again, Perish the thought!'

Do I seem too anti-competitive to you, Kâzim? – Feel free to tell me. – Out with it, if that's the case! – Please! You don't need to act the modest civilian-service type with me. Do you think I'm doting, maybe? – You're an odd one, Kâzim.

You don't let anyone look any deeper. There's no way you are as simple as you make out.

Like watchmaker Wenk with his numb hands, I too grew up in an age when it was drummed into people that they had to be able to do something. A terrible, terrible thing it was to miss out on your career – all those kinds of warnings. I remember the story, part of my preparation for Confirmation, about the man who entrusted his property to his servants, and then condemned the one servant who had buried his talent beneath the earth, where it couldn't generate further talents. Human beings must take advantage of every minute and not drift around, aimlessly, in the world God created. We would like so much to be free, but have hardly acquitted ourselves of one duty when we start to tailor our next corset.

If I describe my own personal town walk to Frau Lüscher-Stucki, and she wipes the sweat from her brow with a lilac cloth and says, all agitated, 'I'd never manage anything as arduous as that!', then I get to work on her.

I say, 'If you turn your mind to walking, then simply don't worry about performance. You shouldn't compare yourself to others. In walking, there is no victory over others, and no such thing as defeat. You aren't competing with anyone, Frau Lüscher-Stucki. Competing with others is a torture rack. Competition is a relentless sieve.'

Walkers don't set out to do a more difficult walk than someone else. That wouldn't be a benchmark for their art. They don't set out to climb two hundred metres, or to do fifteen hundred metres in six minutes. Those are the types of goals sportsmen set themselves. Those who want to beat others, or themselves, do sport.

I lost my brother early in life. Just as an example. Our friends, my brother and I decided to race to see who would be the quickest to get to Marktgasse, the street where we all lived. Matthäus – in his sweat-drenched, red-checked shirt – was the exhausted victor. At home, he turned on the tap, let the water run a good while, so it was really cold and refreshing, then drank a jugful in one go. A week later, he'd bad pneumonia. Within a month, he was dead.

Thirteen, my brother was. A stroke of fate you can't come to terms with, unless you accept it. Even nowadays, I sometimes think I can hear his voice, imagine I can see him, in the Day Room or the Dining Room, behind a curtain where he so liked to hide.

For days, Father didn't say a word. He just squeezed Mother's arm constantly as if he were suffering a physical pain.

'If you don't want to, you don't have to go to the funeral, Lukas,' Mother said.

'But I'd like to go – with you both.' – Father clasped my hand as if he were being lacerated.

The evening before the start of the summer holidays, I told Father I wanted to go and see Grandfather, the village schoolteacher in Schüpfen.

Father was standing at the front door, smoking.

'Come here, Lukas,' he said, his voice as toneless as the wind.

I was standing beside him, but he didn't say a word. I lowered my head, and he continued smoking. Finally, he said, 'Go to bed, Lukas.'

I squeezed past and his elbow brushed my arm. He stepped inside after me and said, casually, 'Let's eat early tomorrow. We'll go to the cemetery together.'

At the door of the room, he turned and looked at me. His cigarette was smouldering in the darkness. He cleared his throat and said again, 'Go to bed, Lukas.'

For a moment he stood there in silence, then I saw the glow of his cigarette turn away from me.

I said, 'Dad, I'd like to go and see Grandfather.'

At that point, he came over and put his hand on my hair. 'We'll talk about it tomorrow.'

I couldn't get to sleep for a long time. My father appeared before my eyes, sitting in the middle of a white, empty surface, on an apple crate.

I wouldn't like to forget everything. To eat my soup with a fork. To cut my ears off. The year before last, Herr Ruchti, a wise, friendly man, started being forever on the move, around the building, laughing quietly to himself, looking for things. And yet you'd the impression that what he was looking for was in his pocket. One morning, he couldn't find his electric razor. Smiling, he asked Frau Lüscher-Stucki did she have it, but she didn't. Did she know where it had got to? She didn't. Could he maybe borrow *her* shaving things? Frau Lüscher-Stucki had to remind him she doesn't use shaving things. Herr Ruchti was transferred to the special-care home in Holenacker. Panorama, it's called. I miss him terribly.

A quarter of all those over eighty lose their minds. I try to keep my mind alert. For decades, thoughts to and fro like weaver's shuttles; then they suddenly decelerate. The first to disappear are the names, then the nouns. I need scissors and say to Irina in the Gift-Making Group, 'Can you please let me have the . . . oh . . . eh . . . drat, the things for cutting.'

You become slow, quiet, then turn into a lettuce-head. Recently, I've been wondering more and more whether I'll still be living here in a year's time. I'm full of concern: how long will I still be able to speak, hear, perceive things? How long will I still be able to sense, for example, that my son is with me, that I'm not alone. The end of my path is becoming more and more identifiable. I've started taking my leave of people, but they tell me it's still too early for that. Angela dreams aloud about all the things she wants to show me in the south of France. What, Kâzim? – I thought you said something.

Should I tell you something? I've researched this thoroughly over a long period of time, and there are a great many examples of scientists, musicians and poets finding surprising solutions for their problems while out for a walk. Quite unexpectedly, the solutions came to them at the edge of meadows, in rambling gardens or on forest paths.

Take the discovery of the molecular structure of benzene. For years, the chemist August Kekulé tried without success to discover the structure of benzene. A closed ring of carbon atoms, do you remember, Kâzim? On a windy evening in 1865, sick of the crackling fire in the hearth, Kekulé goes outside. The leaves of a birch tree dance before his eyes. Forms in various different designs. Leaves and branches, moving, twining and twisting in snake-like motion. But what's this? One of the snakes seizes hold of its own tail, and the form whirls mockingly before Kekulé's eyes. In a flash, he understands and spends the rest of the night . . . – Frau Dürig, how are you? Did you try the hot milk and bread I recommended to you? – So, how was it? Tasty? – You see! Full of strange vitamins. – No. Tomorrow, I have to attend a funeral. A close friend of my late Emilie. – Yes, the country's dying out. If I'm asked what I do, I answer: I go to funerals. – I've developed firm principles for funerals, principles I adhere to strictly. – Why, yes. I position myself at a table, find a reliable waitress who will look after me, and receive the people. Ever since I passed the eighty mark, it seems too much like hard work, much too tiring, to have to push my way through crowds of mourners. – Your woollen coat's at the laundry? – You won't need it, don't worry. A hood or umbrella, at most. – This is Kâzim, our new carer. Gentle and shy. You have to keep asking him to speak up. He clears his throat and says 'Sorry', then carries on mumbling as before. – How did you guess, Frau Dürig? – Someone has to encourage the others. In the entire civilised world there's a need for more walkers. The United States of North America need walkers. Russia needs walkers. North Korea could do with a few. – Why, yes. It's my task to get people out onto the streets and give them a little shove. – I'll knock on your door the day after tomorrow then. Gladly. – Until then, Frau Dürig, you too!

Or take the composer Giuseppe Tartini. Not heard of him? Has a walk to thank for his Devil's Trill Sonata. In his study, Tartini reads the Faust legend. Then heads out to stretch his legs in the park. The devil steps out from behind a pine, with a violin in his hand, and plays eerie, odd notes, full of peculiar trills and fast runs. In his memoirs, Tartini tells us how astonished he was at hearing the devil play with such virtuosity. Tartini hurries home. He shoves the violin beneath his chin, replays what he heard and presents the work as his own. Look at Frau Dürig and you'd be forgiven for thinking the slightest breeze would knock her off her feet. A wounded little bird, fallen to the ground. Her deceased husband was the exact opposite. Herr Dürig's wonderfully broad shoulders are something you, sadly, Kâzim, won't now get to behold. He died on his sixty-second wedding anniversary.

Frau Dürig, so petite. Herr Dürig, broad and bearded. Both were from large families, had lived through hard times. After the war, Herr Dürig didn't succeed in finding the well-paid job he needed to look after his mother and two invalid siblings. In his despair, he wrote to the fortress commander under whom he'd served in a secret tunnel in Mount Lötsch and who now held some thankless, local position in Berne. The commander promised to get him a job with the Municipal Transport Authority, but he'd have to come for interview. Herr Dürig couldn't afford the train fare, so he cycled on a rattly old single-speed from Frutigen in the Kander Valley to the capital. There, he dusted his clothes off and entered the ministry building on Eigerplatz. You'd have looked at him as astonished as I was when it dawned on you he'd cycled back the same day, but Herr Dürig would just have blinked at Frau Dürig and said, 'It wasn't at all taxing. I had the promise of a job, after all, and on a piece of paper the name of a beguiling office miss I'd come across in the anteroom.'

Not long ago, here in the Home, I got to meet one of Frau Dürig's many sons-in-law. A good-humoured, well-nourished man, with a file under his arm. 'Herr Zbinden, it's really nice that you're encouraging my ailing mother-in-law to get out into the fresh air. Here's a hundred-franc note for taking the trouble. No, don't be embarrassed, my expenses will cover it.'

I ask him, 'And you yourself? Do you go for walks?'

'No, no, I've too much to do.'

You understand: a good chap, but as far removed from the solutions to chemical or musical problems as the earth is from Uranus.

I knew many people who said, rightly, 'I'm a grafter. And I'm exhausted.' With great fervour, they sought honorary posts, activities to be involved in; demonstrated their endurance levels without so much as a blink; rushed with import and export figures to meetings and conferences in the remotest of settlements, gasping like some creature in labour. And then death came along and they discovered: they'd spent the voyage across the sea in the ship's hold. Hadn't seen: the ocean beneath a starry sky; the coasts, crowned with piers and stinking harbours; the inhospitable islands, smoking volcanoes. Not heard the seagulls screeching. Not scratched crusted salt from the planks. Never thrown a lifebelt to a drowning man. They didn't know what they were so angry about, and didn't know how to calm themselves. Nightmarish. Buried alive. But you don't have to live like that. Going for a walk takes you up on deck.

Do you know what my son once said? 'If you've seen one wave, Dad, you've seen them all.'

In the Zbinden family, there was no history of conscientious objection to walking until my son came along. Who have you learned this habit from, Kâzim? Of putting your free hand in your pocket?

I can hardly think of a single trait that Markus might have inherited from me. Are we completely different men? I could never have cuddled him the way he was later to cuddle his child. Markus took the whining bundle and rocked her gently, to and fro, murmuring all the while, to calm her down. Thirty years earlier, I wouldn't even have pushed the pram across the square outside the church. Lullabies, I rattled off as if they were cavalry charges. Infants that had to spend the day with me were so homesick they fell ill. Markus, on the other hand, changed his daughter's nappy, made her porridge, took her to the doctor, sat down beside her and read to her. How could he work and at the same time always get up in the night to comfort his teething daughter? Even on workdays, he played hide-and-seek and tig with her at the playground. If she went into a rage, threw herself on the floor and kicked her legs in the air, he knew how to calm his wife as well as their daughter. If Angela held her hand-made teddy out of their third-floor window, waving it to teach it how to fly, he would let her. Markus didn't snatch the bear from her hand, didn't give her a real ticking-off, just said calmly, 'But don't let go until I tell you. I don't think he's quite got the hang of it yet.'

I always had to coerce my son into carrying our mineral water delivery down into the cellar. To his daughter, he said one day, 'Angela, I bet a big strong girl like you can carry that crate down on your little finger' – and from that moment on, he didn't have to ask.

In my day, I'd give Markus a clout. No, I did, I did. I had to explain to him that it could have dire consequences for him if he poked a piece of wire into an electric socket. I thought I could see in his face that he'd try again at the first opportunity, so I slapped him one and reiterated that putting wire in a socket could be very, very sore.

As a boy, Markus loved going to the airport. From the observation terrace, we would watch reverently as planes took off and landed. Shoulder to shoulder, we studied the flight information on the boards. Viewed, noisily, the displays in the kiosks and shops. As strangers, what would we take away from here? We observed the passengers, the staff, the porters. How do holidaymakers differ from business travellers? Are the group travellers already speaking to each other, or still standing some distance apart? Is the family there to welcome the man who puts the food on the table out of a sense of duty or because they can't wait to see him again? We imagined we were returning from Tokyo or Zanzibar, or flying to Brazil, and felt some of the excitement we sensed around us. As I lifted Markus to let him see a plane landing, Emilie and I tried to fathom the logic of those parents who will never board a plane together. Would you rather be on the plane that doesn't make it? Or prefer to be the one left alone, bringing up your son on a small allowance?

Later, we often fought, and more than once Emilie reprehended me. 'You know, Lukas, you're one of those people who always interferes. If Markus brings friends home to listen to records, you simply take over. He can't get a word in. That must be terribly annoying for him.'

Was I a bad father? I came to his defence against Emilie when he came home at night later than agreed, but if I hoped to hear about it, I was disappointed. When I asked 'How was it?' he would answer 'Fine', and that was it. If Emilie asked whom he'd met and who had said what, he happily told her.

At sixteen, he attended dancing lessons in Interlaken every Thursday night. Frau Spycher would play a certain chord on her piano, and the girls would rise, stand before their chairs and wait for the boys to ask them to dance. Normally, Markus chose Rhea Gugger, from Ringgenberg. Emilie and I couldn't understand why, wasn't she bigger than him? Emilie discovered the reason, 'He likes her eau de cologne. *4711*.'

When I'd asked, he'd just shrugged his shoulders.

It's like drawing teeth if I want something out of him.

'How was your day, Markus?'

'Mm.'

'Anything new?'

'Nothing.'

And later, Emilie informs me that Rhea Gugger finished with him after the final lesson. I give a loud groan. 'Is that "nothing"?' Incredible.

Could you bear to see your child be sad, Kâzim? You hope you'd be able to chase away the sadness by immediately doing or saying the right thing. I could never bear being in the same room if my son's face took on that unhappy expression. As a father, you feel responsible. Fated to deal with it.

'You need to go out,' I called across to him, from the doorway of his room. 'And get to know your friends' sisters' girl friends.'

'Yeah, yeah.' Markus lies on his bed, with a tortured look, staring at the ceiling.

'If you can make a woman laugh, people say, you're halfway there.'

Markus is silent.

'According to Emilie, the best way to deal with a broken heart is to take an axe and split wood until you drop with exhaustion.'

'Mama never had a broken heart.'

'I'm trying to give you ideas, at least. Don't you have any of your own?'

'Do you know what, Dad?' He straightens up. 'Life is some shit illness I managed to catch somewhere.'

'Maybe you are your own shit illness?'

The door to his room slams in my face. And yet, believe me, I was about to take him in my arms until everything was all right again. But Markus shuts himself in.

Here, look, a letter from my granddaughter, with questions about how I am, with news of what she's doing in her spare time. 'Don't always ask the same question, Granda, you'll be the first to know if I'm leaving for Marseille. You can count on that.'

Enclosed with the letter was a post-it from Markus, telling me to ask the administration in the Home for a form he needs for his tax declaration.

My son and I: we're grown men with our own, independent experiences. Surely, it should now be possible for us to speak to each other. It's just that when he has to make the long journey down to the entrance hall with me, it's as if his mouth has been tied shut. I ask why he's not telling me anything, and he says, 'It's not that I'm keeping anything from you. It's simply that Verena and Angela and I get on well, and there's nothing to tell.'

'And at work?'

'Pages and pages are copied out of my scientific articles. So I've reason to be happy.' He then falls silent again.

And as for the opposite: how can walkers walk past it all – suffering, misery, begging, pollution – and not do anything? A pyromaniac bursts into a primary school with a box of matches? And Zbinden the Walker? What does he do to ensure such a thing never happens again? Does he deliberately blind himself to the seriousness of the international situation? Just recently, one nation marched out of its own country and into another with a worse balance of trade. Does Zbinden the Walker hear the resulting discord? Or does he harbour the illusion that the world's in a hopeless situation, anyway, it's *drowning* in hopelessness, and there are far too few lifebelts for the number of people drowning? That the way the world's cereals are distributed is, quite simply, irreversible? Does he blind himself to the thought that history should move in the direction of improvement, and human beings, grow to attain greater freedom and perfection? Or does he regard the question of women, the starving, the persecuted, in terms of 'job done!'? As for the exploitation of man by his fellow man – on whose side does a walker see himself? Don't you ask yourself these questions, Kâzim? – You *do*?

Take the year 1776. Austria abolishes torture. America declares its independence. James Cook sails round the world for the third time. The first living orang-utan is brought to Holland. And the unworldly walker is sitting in Eisenstadt, wondering whether to cut his toenails or buy a larger size of boot.

My granddaughter likes to bad-mouth walkers as aesthetes and utopians with no ambitions. She can, indeed, identify valuable elements in a walk, she says, from which people could build a knowledgeable world experience, but she slates walkers for not going about this productively enough. The fruits of their efforts? The visible use? Critics of walking view walking, on the whole, as a form of diversion. And all diversions, as is well known, and as Pascal said, are nothing but a human invention to ensure we avoid seeing the enormous suffering beneath the horror of our own unfathomable misery. But Heraclitus – does the name mean anything to you, Kâzim? Slept on a dung-hill to cure himself of dropsy and spoke about how, even when asleep, we contribute, directly or indirectly, to what goes on in the world. This is the sense, I explain to my granddaughter, in which walkers operate too.

You know, I regard walkers as pioneers in the battle for freedom of movement and like to see them as friends of free movement across the world, and yet – on one point, I share the view of my critics: when it comes to appointing people to posts in government, preference should be given to single-minded motorists. Politics, as you know, comes down to being in the right place at the right time. There, behind us. Can you hear that, Kâzim? The manager's coming crashing towards us. His key ring rattling and dancing on his belt. – Did Herr Probst find you, Herr Stauffer? – One moment, Herr Stauffer! Is the rumour true that you want to fire the chef and have a canteen kitchen deliver our food? – Whoa!

Now tell me, Kâzim! Is that his idea of sheltered housing? Could he not at least have stopped briefly and asked how we are? He could have badgered you with questions about your first week here, or said hello, at least. What are you looking for down there, Kâzim? – Oh. – Emilie used to tie her laces calmly and without rushing – compared to you. Are you happy with your laces? – Without the right laces, the leather doesn't shine as it should. Do you not think the laces a little too shiny? – I think they're a little too shiny. Why don't you do a double knot?

Maybe I should give her a holiday. – My granddaughter. Where would you like to travel to, Kâzim?

Always untroubled, inclined to be cheerful, Emilie would be asleep almost before her head had touched the pillow. She got up early, was always active, always in excellent form, ate light meals, no meat, two pills per annum. She should've lived to be a hundred. It would interest me to know what position the Federal Health Ministry would take regarding Emilie's death.

'Emilie, do you never worry?' I would ask her.

'I have a low opinion of worrying.'

'I can't believe you're never worried. I worry about Markus, I torture myself thinking he could get into difficulty. I wouldn't be a good father if I didn't do that – correct? Yesterday, biting this Benjamin boy – what on earth's wrong with him?'

'Nothing, you fool. He's just very active: active and bright.'

'I worry about my work. If I don't take work seriously, I'll lose it. I worry about the situation in the world, the governments couldn't care less about things. We plan a picnic, and I worry we could be rained off. I worry about you, about your well-being, though you don't appreciate that at all. Not to worry is like escaping, a way of shirking your responsibility, of suppressing all your problems and not giving a damn about everything else.'

Emilie laughed out loud. 'I once tried to worry. As you worry about everything, I thought I might be missing out on something. I decided a certain day would be my worry day – to find out what it's all about. That morning, I refused to get up, pulled the cover over my head, and you asked was I pregnant again? I kicked the duvet aside: nine o'clock, that explained the brightness in the room. I refused to do any kind of work and read the newspaper. One article was about how, in the US, big business and the military were as good as married. I made every effort to worry until lunchtime, but couldn't do it. I gave up early.'

'How do you manage that?'

'By trusting.'

'Trusting? Trusting in what? In whom? Can trusting make worries vanish?'

'Maybe not,' said Emilie, 'but it helps to get over them. At least, they don't bother you so much then.'

You're asking yourself what Emilie meant by trusting, Kâzim? Believe me, I've been asking myself that longer than you. I mull it over like Herr Ziegler's archaeologists would an unknown hieroglyphic. Sometimes I think my wife existed to show me what was beyond me.

Herr Probst! Did you get anywhere on the top floor? Threaten to go on hunger strike? – At least the manager raced past us there, like a startled hare. – Stick to your guns, whatever you do. I once knew a very old, uncouth man who gave the person delivering his meals a chain of human molars. But that was many moons ago and is a very old yarn. – This evening? – Pardon? – No, Herr Pfammatter isn't here, no, I think he's gone to Budapest . . . – What? – I hope not, but of course I can't . . . – No, I don't know whether Herr Hügli is available. We'll see, Herr Probst. – Yes, lie down for a while.

Herr Probst never admits when he has a hangover. But there are days when he says he's pretty tired, and today is one of those days.

You're bound to run into Herr Pfammatter, Kâzim. He's travelling at the moment. Once a year, the travel bug gets to him. Then he jumps into his best suit and puts a beret on. He stuffs a pullover, rainwear, his toothbrush and some cracked soap into a battered grey army rucksack and, with the straps of a camera, a map case and binoculars tied round him, sets off for some distant destination. He looks like René Gardi, the folklorist, who spends his year in the savanna surrounded by giraffes, wildebeests and Masai spears.

Last Friday, in the corridor, he said to me, beaming, 'It's good I've seen you, Herr Zbinden, I'm off to Budapest today for four days. Would you please inform the management once I've gone? They might be alarmed otherwise.'

Without stolen souvenirs, Pfammatter's travels would be unthinkable. You can look forward to seeing his room, Kâzim! Full of curious objects – the most valuable, and all the fragile ones, he keeps on the top shelf so Hügli's tom can't get anywhere near. From a café in Saint-Germain-des-Prés,

Herr Pfammatter brought back the Gitanes ashtray; from a trip on the *Wiener Walzer* overnight train, the sign saying Zurich–Vienna. In the National Park, he slipped a 225-million-year-old stone fossil into his rucksack. A fully rigged ship in a bottle. A silver snuffbox, decorated with fine twines and flourishes. A block of sandstone – wherever he got that from. Property isn't what belongs to you, he makes out. Property is what you can keep from other people.

These thefts are quickly put into perspective when you consider all the things Herr Pfammatter leaves behind on his travels: hairbrushes, cultural guides, the return portions of his tickets. On his last-but-one trip, he ended up in Rome. There, he told us once he was back, an incredible urge for a bowl of milky coffee came over him, the kind of milky coffee you can dip your bread into. Pfammatter sat himself down in a bar, ordered milky coffee, and asked for milky coffee again when the waiter brought him just a coffee in a thimble-sized cup. Pfammatter whipped out a pencil, took the serviette and drew a coffee cup with two ears, the kind used in the early nineteenth century. At the top, he drew some steam and wrote the word *caffè*. The waiter took the espresso back to the counter, took a soup bowl from the cupboard, and pulled the lever twelve times. But what's Herr Pfammatter supposed to do with a dozen espressos in a soup bowl? So he draws a cow on the serviette and with both hands, four fingers clasping the thumbs, imitates a farmer milking over the coffee. The waiter rushes back and brings over two little jugs of milk that Pfammatter, now satisfied, pours into his coffee.

'Rome is hellishly expensive,' he complained, trying to fix his camera in the Day Room. 'Twenty-eight euros, that coffee cost me.'

Herr Pfammatter couldn't get the flap on the camera to open, the flap over the battery compartment for the light meter. We tried to screw it open with a coin, but – no hope – the flap refused to budge. The shutter was crooked, having been screwed on badly, and the threads weren't catching. Herr Furrer, a retired engineer, kept us company as we tried, and explained in great detail how Herr Pfammatter could take photos even without a light meter. He'd only have to adjust the shutter settings of the lens depending on the light conditions, and do so in keeping with the scale on the instruction leaflet that came with the film. Though I knew no person in his right mind would ever use this method, Herr Pfammatter listened patiently. Later, when my family came by on a Sunday visit, I asked Herr Pfammatter to give his camera to my son. Markus disappeared to my room and returned with it repaired an hour and a half later. I remarked to the ever-so-pleased and grateful Herr Pfammatter, 'I knew Markus would relish the challenge.'

'Above all,' my daughter-in-law objected, 'if he can help someone in doing so.'

It was one of those moments when I can see that I don't know my son at all, but perhaps we should talk about Markus another time.

From Rome? In St Peter's Basilica he took a candle socket down off the wall. – But of course. Herr Pfammatter really has to check himself in order not to steal here in the Home. The building's crammed with all kinds of junk. Trinkets, Persian carpets, the amphora vase with the spray of golden dwarf broom in the Day Room.

What's the point of our being alive, Kâzim? – To fulfil a task? But that's precisely the difficulty! What is the task? In strictest confidence: as a teacher I corrected jotters every evening, but if all that had gone up in smoke, not a single tear would have been shed. The pupils corrected one error with a new error; and, jeering, at the end of their schooldays, threw their exercise sheets, crumpled into balls, into a cement mixer to prove how I had failed. Thank Heaven I lived to see my retirement. At last I could be free-and-easy when out and about on Seidenfadenstrasse, and didn't need to fear snowball peltings from the balconies of blocks of flats. What I'm saying is: for most people, teachers are, and knowledge is, completely useless. Unless it's for the entertainment value. If a piece of knowledge is neither funny nor scary, and if it's not going to make you rich, then ditch it. I'm sure you were a good pupil, Kâzim. Hardly home from school before you were sitting down to your homework. No TV until your homework was done – am I right?

But 'task' in what sense? In the past, you often saw death notices in the papers with a terrible quotation over them: 'Your work was your life, you never thought of yourself. Looking after your kin was your greatest duty.' Every time I read that, I thought, 'That's an obituary for a brewery horse.'

I don't think the purpose of being here is to fulfil a task. Civilian service – instead of military – fine, and if you help old people on staircases, that isn't bad either. But if the old person doesn't know the point of being alive, then surely you can't know whether it makes sense to help him. In that case, you're maybe better sitting him down, stripped to the waist, at an open window, and he'll be dead before supper. – No? – You can discuss these things endlessly.

What's the point of being alive? You know, my grandparents' home was always there for me. Once, I was sitting in my grandfather's study, reading with grim determination.

'Granda, what does this mean?' I ask. 'This here. Is that English?'

I carry the book over to Grandfather who is seated, sad-eyed, at his desk. He takes the book from me and clears his throat. '*To Look and Pass* is the title. See and die.' He gives the book back to me and glances at me, watchfully, over the top of his steel-rimmed glasses. 'Now, Lukas, have you any idea what could be meant by that?'

'Yes, Granda, I think so. See and die. Maybe other people see it differently, but for me it means: you are born, live and die. You look at the thing and pass on. It doesn't matter whether you work or not, make something of yourself or remain a zero, whether you run around madly or stand still.' I look at the book. 'Matthäus looked at everything and died,' I say, quietly.

I clearly remember the odd silence that followed these words.

'Now, Lukas,' Grandfather puts his glasses on the table and rubs his eyes, 'where would we be if everyone thought like that? Where would we be without ambition, without get-up-and-go, without striving for justice?'

He smiles weakly and puts a hand on my shoulder. He tries to continue speaking, but doesn't.

'Sometimes I think I'm to blame for his death,' I say. 'If I hadn't been so determined to beat him, he wouldn't have raced down the alley like a savage.'

'You mustn't think like that,' Grandfather says.

'It's just: I miss Matthäus.'

'I miss him too.' Then Grandfather takes his bowler and his stick and leaves the room to go for his daily walk.

Do you know what I think, Kâzim? We're not walkers by nature but are in the world to become walkers. To touch trees with winter-proof leaves. To rub wild rosemary and thyme between our fingers and smell them. Let sand slip through our fingers. To pet the coats of dogs that won't bark, never mind bite. To take a new path to the Day Room every day. Let wild strawberries, warm from the sun, melt on your tongue, and smell the pine resin. And if a person isn't interested in such things, he's missed his calling as a human being. Then there's no point in talking to him about all kinds of possible and impossible things.

I'm telling you that because it's a great comfort. Although you can never really know what use words are. It's been known to happen that I've talked about walking, and the listeners tell me: your words are boring. Am I boring you,

Kâzim? If it's boring, it's my fault. Walkers can sometimes put you off walking.

I'm thinking of a particular day when Emilie and I walked through Bonstetten Park in Thun, where there were gigantic Canadian firs. Barefoot along the gravel path, careful not to step on a broken bottle. I talked the whole time, for some reason. In flowery language, I outlined everything I knew. I wanted to impress Emilie. And now, hold your breath. Emilie pulls her silk shawl tighter round her shoulders. And suddenly, out of nowhere, this gentle woman turns to me and slaps me across the face!

My lip was bleeding and there were tears in my eyes. I looked at Emilie, indignant, put my hand up to my lip and said, 'That's the limit! Why did you do that?'

You didn't often get the opportunity to voice your indignation with her. I gave it my best shot. And with a vehemence I'd never before experienced from her, she shouted, 'Just be quiet for once!'

Emilie and I had survived a war, brought a child into the world, spooned soup from the same tureen, comforted each other at the funerals of our respective parents, stood by one another in sickness and in health. And now, all of a sudden, she was a transformed woman. Calmer, she added, 'Just shut your mouth for once, Lukas.'

Now, Emilie was no doubt right. All in all, she was a good bit cleverer than me. But I also had my pride. 'Very well,' I began. 'Stevenson did write that marriage was one long conversation, but if you like, I'll never say anything ever again.'

The whole of the next day, I remained silent. Anything I had to communicate went down in writing. My teacher colleagues were frightened by my silence, believe me. For my pupils, I was a lost case. Would you say you're capable of being silent, Kâzim? – I look every pupil in the eye briefly, sit down, fold my arms and cross my legs. The pupils, too, try to sit as comfortably as possible, shift on their seats for a while still, rest their arms on the scuffed desks or their legs. Some look at the teacher, others look around, silently consulting their neighbours, give cautious smiles. The classroom becomes quiet. We sit and wait. Nothing happens. I'm still sitting in the same position and there's no sign of my being about to break the silence. Martin is the first to show the strain. He can't sit still any more, his upper body leans forward, then he sits back again, he coughs and snaps a rubber in two. Others lose patience too, chair-shifting, Fredy and Kurt grin at each other, the girls giggle. In the back row, a sharpener falls to the floor. Five minutes have already passed without anyone saying anything. Martin leans forward on both elbows and addresses a question to me. 'Herr Zbinden, how long is this going to go on for?'

His voice sounds tinny after the long silence. He clears his throat and repeats the question. The others are startled, look to me, but I don't answer. I change the position of my legs, look around the group.

Martin now addresses the other pupils. 'If the teacher doesn't want to, then we'll just start without him.' And when no one does, he adds, 'Why's no one saying anything? It's not as if he's forbidden us to speak, he's just not speaking himself. Let him be quiet, what does it matter to us?'

He nods in my direction, but without looking at me. Now the others start to relax. They begin to speak, all at once; if the teacher doesn't want to, then we just will, that's what we're here for, isn't it, okay, let's get started, but they don't quite know what to start with. As each suggestion is made, they look in my direction, hoping I'll nod in agreement.

In a fluster, Martin turns to me and says, 'This is not on, Herr Zbinden.'

The others look at me, full of expectation.

'I suggest we take out our Geography books, and Konrad reads something out,' Silvia says. She looks at me, waiting.

'Has anyone any objections?' Martin asks.

'Why Konrad?' Mathilda asks.

'You read then,' says Martin.

Konrad sits and sulks as if something's been taken away from him. He pulls a face.

'What do I have to read?' Mathilda asks, looking at me.

'Something that will interest everybody,' Martin says.

'That's boring as shit, if you ask me,' says Konrad.

'Shut your gob, you!' Martin screams, throwing half a rubber at him. 'Mathilda, kindly read to us!' He looks round the class. 'No one has any objections. So let us begin.'

'What do you mean: no one has any objections?' Konrad says, and a ruler flies through the air. 'Some people haven't said anything yet!'

'We're stuck on the moon without any bog paper,' Fredy pipes up, with a grin, while Martin and Konrad lay into each other – each questions the other's mental abilities, casts a slur on the legitimacy of the other's birth, and there's a barrage of foul expressions, highlighting activities ranging from incest to intercourse with barn animals.

'Konrad! Martin! That's enough!' the teacher shouts, reaching for the blackboard pointer and slamming it down on his desk.

It's perhaps not the most favourable moment to break my silence. For Martin and Konrad show no intention of stopping. They pounce on each other, Martin sits on Konrad's chest . . . What do you mean, Kâzim? *Cruel?* You think I was cruel to my pupils? – Listen, I taught in a catchment area where the people were cruel, believe me. Konrad's hosing the skinny chickens down, they're clucking and flapping around. 'Why are you doing that?' I call across to him.

Konrad shouts, 'Because chickens hate water!'

Konrad lay in wait for Martin behind the fire brigade station and gave him a doing, leaving the bridge of his nose in bits, but Emilie supported me in my plan to introduce regular silence days. – Frau Jacobs, your visitors have left already? – And your itch, it's still itching? – Exactly. You need to get Lydia to give you some milking grease. – I meant to ask you earlier, how's your brother, the one in hospital? – What do you mean, they let him out again? What do they think he is, a lion? – Get Lydia to . . . Okay! – Bye!

She's noticed you, Kâzim, Frau Jacobs is acknowledging you. A good start, congratulations. – I know. The entire team doesn't like Frau Jacobs especially. The chef goes out of his way to find a fresh peach for her, and hopes in vain she won't notice the marks on it. In the past, you should realise, her name was well known. People talked about her over lunch, at the garden fence. 'Have you seen Julia Jacobs in this new film?'

Ask Frau Jacobs whether she's still recognised in the street. She'll tell you, honestly, that she doesn't like to be recognised, and likes it even less *not* to be recognised. She'll admit quite freely that her talent was founded on youth and beauty, neither of which she now possesses. Her name was known in the Elysée Palace and amid the ice of Norway. – But no, of course, she doesn't think she's superior, somehow. She has requests she makes to the staff, and the staff make requests back. – Why so impatient? She's afraid of being transferred, at some point, to a special-care home. Sedated by medication. Kept there against her wishes. And silenced.

A nice little town but a terrible catchment area, believe me. Once, Emilie wanted to take Konrad's mother to a women's meeting across the bridge in Interlaken. Carlotta. She needed to get out more, Emilie reckoned. Carlotta's husband wasn't happy with her going, simply loved causing trouble. But Emilie said, 'Just don't take it from him, Carlotta. Say hello from me – what kind of country does he think we live in?'

Carlotta worked on her husband and, finally, was permitted to go. They met up with Annemarie and Frau Schmutz and I don't know who else in the Savoy. They were talking and laughing, and it got really late. Well after midnight it was, when Emilie took Carlotta home, to Hohmüedig.

Emilie went in with her to have a last coffee. And Carlotta's husband's sitting in front of the TV. Raging, he looks at his wife, jumps up and hits her in the face – so hard she falls over. He then makes for Emilie who runs away.

No, he did, he wanted to belt her one too. Maybe he thought he'd be doing me a favour. Emilie was raving and ranting when she got home. I was long since in bed. She rushed up to me, pulled me up and hugged me. She calmed down and I said, 'Come on, we'll sit down and you can tell me what happened.'

When she was finished, it was my turn to jump up, raving and ranting, to put on my shirt and trousers, and run to the police station in Marktgasse. They listened and nodded, but no one wanted to go and fetch Carlotta's husband to take his fingerprints. So, taking bigger steps than usual, I stomped my way to Carlotta's house, hammered at the door and, when the door was opened, set upon her husband. 'You belong in jail,' I shouted.

He put up his hands to protect his face. Konrad tried to grab my arms and tear me away from his father. In her nightdress, Carlotta was shouting, with a burst lip, 'Thomas! Your teeth. Watch your teeth!'

The incident left its mark on me too, and Emilie put poultices on the injured body parts. 'Konrad still hasn't seen a man who can get by without turning violent,' she said.

My heart hurts if I think of Konrad. The circumstances he's grown up in. What will have become of him meanwhile?

An eternally long staircase, God knows. You'd think I was Methuselah's age, the way I'm taking these steps. I need longer to go down these stairs than it takes a lazy Christian to get to Paradise. Maybe, in future, I should take the lift after all? You enter it for a few seconds, and meanwhile they're altering the world outside.

Let's sit down a moment in the alcove there, Kâzim. It's true, Herr Imhof regards this sofa as his private property, but it's the most comfortable seat in the entire Home, imagine! – No, you can't smoke, surely you know it's all no-smoking here, Kâzim? The Home, from top to bottom, is one big oxygen tent. Lydia cowers on the very top landing from time to time, at the door to the attic. It's the only place in this wonderful old building where she can enjoy a cigarette without setting the alarm off.

Sad? What makes you think I could be sad? – I'm just trying not to speak for a while. Federal Councillor Rudolf Minger used, before chairing a public administration meeting or addressing the Agricultural Association, to sit on a comfortable chair, close his mouth, and sleep like a babe in arms for a quarter of an hour. I spent all my lunchtimes trying to do the same, with varying degrees of success. Sure, my life was in no way sensational. I was conscientious and did my work well, but I'm in no way outstanding. My pupils saw no danger, shine or reason to get excited in me. I'm an ordinary man and have lived an ordinary life. I've taken paths, no doubt, many others took before me. On the other hand, I loved someone, with all my heart and soul, and that was always enough for me.

But the writers are right: love makes you suffer. During our walk round the shops on the main street, one morning, Emilie vanished from my side all of a sudden. I heard a loud sigh. Then it was as if the ground had swallowed her up. Straight away, a nice, somewhat nervous-seeming man addressed me, and don't ask me how, but I knew right away that this had to be Walter Hensler, Emilie's admirer from the bird-watching course, above Interlaken. Emilie had told me he desperately wanted to take her to the Rex to see a Hitchcock.

'Will you go with him?' I'd enquired, in as composed a fashion as possible.

'Oh, Lukas,' she laughed.

And yet I'm not a jealous man. Anyone who knows Lukas Zbinden well will tell you: I'm not a jealous man. Being smitten, occasionally, is part of life, after all. Nothing to get worked up about.

'Excuse me,' Hensler was now saying. He took a cigarette from an already open and pretty battered packet. 'Have you got a light?'

'No.'

Clumsily, he put the cigarette back. 'Was that not Emilie? I saw her beside you, but she now seems to have disappeared.'

'Yes, that was Emilie. Emilie Zbinden. Did you wish to speak to her?'

'Indeed.'

I became furious. 'Maybe it's not the right moment. Her husband has an incurable illness, and her son's lying in hospital, paralysed down one side, after a bicycle accident.'

'Oh! Emilie has a family?'

He looked so surprised, I became even more furious. When he'd gone, and Emilie turned up beside me again, I said, 'Where did you suddenly go?'

Emilie blushed like a peony. 'Into that shop. I bought terrible glitter wool I'll never be able to use. Expensive, it was, into the bargain. Is he away?'

'Why haven't you told him you're married?' I checked she was wearing her ring.

'Didn't I tell you: he's not asked a single question. Instead, he holds endless lectures about budgerigars. In the heat of midday, budgerigars sit in the shade of the leaves in trees and bushes. Protected by the group, some grab forty winks, with their heads under their wings. Others preen each other's feathers in places they can't reach themselves.'

'You observe budgerigars, above Interlaken?'

'No, but that didn't stop him sharing his knowledge with me. At least, now I know all there is to know about budgies that can't fly and still-dependent nestlings.'

'He's laid his heart at your feet.'

'In an irresistible manner.'

Watch – he doesn't say a word, Kâzim. You try in vain to get him to move his lips. He's not in the habit of greeting others, so don't take it personally. Herr Ziegler! Come over here a moment, I'd like to introduce someone to you. – Our new carer. Kâzim. – His first week here. – Exactly, you said it. Even from the way he leads you downstairs, you can sense his openness. Very skilled at getting people to talk. And you? On your way to the Day Room? – Pardon? – I don't understand that. – You can't get it off? I don't know – the pullover really does seem a little tight. – Try taking your arm out. – Slowly. – Not like that. Wait a moment, from the side. – Can you really not get it off? – Your head is too big and the neck too small, I can see that. What are you laughing at, Kâzim? When we should be helping him. – Patience, Herr Ziegler, try . . . – Why was it necessary to put this pullover on in the first place, Herr Ziegler? What were you thinking of? How come you forced yourself into a pullover without stopping to consider you wouldn't be able to get it off again? – Cut him out with scissors? You must be crazy, Kâzim. – Whatever you think, Herr Ziegler. I wish you success.

Heavens, and I told you he doesn't speak much! That'll teach you to believe what I say about others! But how will he be able to get that pullover off, without damaging himself? Herr Ziegler isn't the first I've seen losing his patience this week. A person I thought was inwardly balanced. On the other hand, a tight pullover would trigger odd feelings in me too. A very tricky one. As for your suggestion, Kâzim, well really! Scissors. Any more of that and I'll think there's something sinister about you. Come on, let's sit down a moment. I'd like to tell you the rest of the Hensler melodrama. Are you sitting comfortably?

After a while, things came to a head. Walter Hensler rushed into the lion's den. He rang the doorbell and I opened the door. I can remember it as if it happened today.

'Good afternoon, Herr Zbinden. My name is Walter Hensler,' he said to introduce himself. 'I'd like to speak to you.'

'We've met before. I believe. I was just preparing a worksheet on Antarctica, but come on in. May I offer you something? Coffee, tea, water?'

'Whatever *you're* having, thanks.'

Hensler had narrow lips and a mysterious mole on his left cheek. His posture betrayed the fact that in his formative years he'd spent hours getting his swinging extremities under control by straightening his back and walking evenly. He was wearing a beige suit, a tie that didn't match, well-worn shoes, and had immaculate manners. He stirred the cream and sugar carefully into his coffee, and smiled cautiously.

'Herr Hensler, do you maybe know why albatrosses migrate with the wind around the Antarctic?'

'Pardon?'

'It's just something I can't get out of my head. What brings you here? Careful, the coffee's hot.'

He placed the coffee spoon, gently, down on the saucer. 'It's to do with your wife.'

'I see.'

He avoided my gaze. 'Emilie. I love her.'

'I see.'

'I'm sorry if I'm catching you unawares with this.'

'Catching? Me?' I said, a little too loudly. 'Why would that be? Why shouldn't you love Emilie. I love her too. She's the best, most intelligent, most fabulous woman on earth. You can sense that, even after motherhood, she has remained a proper woman. Enchanting, devastating, ravishing. The country must be full of men who love her.'

When Emilie and I first met, half a dozen lecherous gardeners were milling round her, for she'd an easy-going manner everyone loved. All those ardent men – on school boards, in reading groups, in amateur choirs – in whom love flared for my wife! Averting your eyes from her was impossible.

'You see, Herr Zbinden, I want to put my cards on the table. For me, it's the only way to prove to myself I'm not a . . . that I'm respectable.' Hensler was speaking in muted fashion, as if asking for forbearance. 'I met Emilie on the bird-watching course. I feel really good when I'm around her.'

'Are you having an affair?'

'Emilie and I? Good God, no!'

'There's nothing going on between you?'

'No!'

'You've put your cards on the table, Herr Hensler,' I said. 'Thank you for that. But why are you speaking to me about this? You're speaking to the wrong person, I reckon.' I forced myself to smile at him, calmly.

Hensler shifted in his seat, less than calmly.

'Let me tell you something, Herr Hensler. When Emilie comes back, we'll ask her straight out: might she maybe be falling in love with you? And which of the two of us would she choose?'

Don't think, Kâzim, that I was taking the matter lightly. Disgruntled, I considered the man, whom Emilie might swap – at any moment – for this touchingly honest, likeable bird-watcher: Lukas Zbinden – reading teaching materials on the sofa, his belt undone to ease the feeling of tightness. His hand beneath his chin, and looking along his face – first, his left cheek, then the right – like in some ridiculous shaving-foam ad. Correcting worksheets, and not making a beeline for her when she comes in the door. His cold feet twitching – always, of course, as she's about to nod off. I wasn't a good husband to her. I didn't drink, it's true, nor did I flirt around. And yet. When had I last surprised her with a gift? Maybe Emilie was lonely, without me noticing? Despite all the choirs she'd joined; despite her job and charity work; the comfort of our son. Maybe, every time I'd not let her finish what she was saying, she'd ground her teeth and told herself – for the umpteenth time, and over how long a period? – 'Give him another chance.' A less patient person would've swapped me for someone else long since.

'Where are you off to, Herr Hensler? Sit down. – *There's someone here for you!*' I called to Emilie as she came in the front door.

'Good evening, Walter,' Emilie said, guardedly. 'What brings you here?'

'Herr Hensler wants to tell you something, Emilie. On you go – tell her.'

Hensler blinked, anxiously. 'I've nothing to say.'

'He'd like to tell you that he worships you. We've agreed you should choose between us.'

'Should what?' asked Emilie.

'Herr Zbinden, that's quite absurd!' Hensler – clearly pained – exclaimed.

'Sit down and join us, Emilie. Would you like a kiss from this person? Yes or no?'

'Lukas, you're annoyed.'

'I'm not annoyed.'

'I'm terribly sorry, Emilie. It's surely better I go . . . ' Hensler gathered his coat together.

'You're going nowhere! You two have things to say to each other. And I'm going to leave you alone. I'm going out to mingle a little. It was a pleasure. Goodbye.'

Outside, with the wind coming straight at me, and my jacket buttoned up to my throat, I immediately let my thoughts distract me. Like some completely inexperienced walker, I was reacting to everything going on inside me. Emilie could leave me. She was a free person. She could leave me whenever she felt like it. Maybe not for a dithery bird-watcher who could talk himself into a flap over budgies. But why always kiss the same lips? She could leave me because she'd answered the questions in a magazine article – *How well do you know your husband?* – only to discover she'd not had to guess a single answer. She could leave me standing with a completely crushed Markus, whose eyes, red from crying, would constantly remind me of her, and of the fact we'd no longer rear him together, within the proper family unit that, until that moment, I'd regarded as permanent. I thought about many things, not least: how unpleasant handing my son over at weekends would be.

A single large raindrop ran across my jacket. A second splashed over the ground, down at my feet. I went home to see if Emilie had already packed her bags.

They were sitting in the living room, drinking tea. He appeared to be telling her something incredibly pleasant, for Emilie seemed incredibly pleased. Her eyes had a dreamy glaze.

'You're back already!' she said.

'There's a storm brewing. But carry on, please carry on. I don't want to disturb you.'

'What have you there, in your hands?'

I handed her what I was carrying, wrapped in brown paper.

'Flowers. Is it a special occasion?'

'Does there need to be a special occasion? It's getting late, Herr Hensler.'

'Yes, of course.' He rose, in measured fashion. 'Goodbye, Emilie.'

'You don't have to rush off.' Emilie gave him a wonderful smile. Not at all the type of smile you give to bird-watching-course acquaintances, if you yourself are happily married. 'Isn't it raining outside? Wait fifteen minutes and let it ease off. If you wish, you can eat with us.'

'I don't think I'd like to,' he said, with a glance in my direction.

'Then at least take one of our umbrellas,' Emilie suggested.

'That's absolutely charming of you, but . . . '

'Take an umbrella.' The way she looked at him was friendly and open. 'Some things in life are given as a gift. You can accept them. It's allowed.'

'Thanks a lot, Emilie.' He actually bowed. 'And thank you for speaking so frankly.'

He pointed the umbrella down as he would a foil, then headed out, into the raging weather.

When my rival in love had vanished, I took a deep breath and sat down beside Emilie.

'He'll *keep* that umbrella,' I said.

'You shouldn't have thrown him out right away like that.'

'I didn't throw him out.'

'It took a lot for him to come here, you know.'

'I see.'

'I'm worried about him.'

'You're worried about him! What did you talk about?'

'Why?'

'Just curious.'

'He proposed to me, and I asked for time to think it over,' Emilie said, sounding like someone about to abandon all the conventions.

'It's okay for you to leave me,' I said, bravely. 'Markus can spend one week with me, one week with you. He'd be annoyed for two years, but then would understand we'd done the right thing. I'd be very happy.'

'You wouldn't be happy.'

'I'd say: on you go, I won't stop you. In the morning, I'd bury my love for you. And in the afternoon, I'd go for a two-hour walk. It's impossible for someone who goes for a walk to feel in any way unhappy. I'd sing as I walked. I'd sing in such a way, dearest, that your heart would break even thinking about it.'

'Told you. You'd be desperately unhappy.'

'I'd explore the terrain, find myself some *terra firma*. A casual affair here, a casual affair there. The women's clothes dropping as I silver-tongue them. I'd even get to feel younger, with some harmless little woman. Not a lot of brain, but well stacked.'

'You're not the type to have affairs, Lukas.'

'Will you be going out with him?'

'He does look pretty good.'

'He has disgusting, piggy eyes.'

'*I* like them. There's a hint of tragedy and mystery about them.'

'Bet he's considering writing your name on his wrist with a piece of glass.'

'Very flattering.'

'Relationships based only on passion have the lowest chance of surviving.'

'I'll take the risk.'

And then a long, intimate kiss: the kind where you struggle for breath, but are unable to move. I can assure you, Kâzim, the cultural gap between a kiss from Valentina and a kiss from Emilie is indescribable. We held each other tight, and the thought came to me, clear as day: that I was in the exact place in the universe where I belonged. Side by side with Emilie. Her hand in mine.

The Walter Hensler story, of course, continued to annoy me. He would phone every few weeks. While Emilie parried his invitations, I thought about ways and means of making it clear to my wife that I wanted to stay with her for a long time still. I decided never again to stuff hankies down the side of the armchair. To replace the loo roll. To put the daily paper away. Maybe Emilie was just as fed up as Frau Wehrli with washing and ironing her husband's shirts? In future, I'd take them to the laundry. I'd give Emilie a cashmere pullover. Perfume. I'd shower her with flowers. Once, from the bathroom, Emilie shouted, 'What's this all about?'

I'd removed the post-it with 'Like yourself anyhow' written on it, and replaced it with '300,000 men covet my wife'.

'That's so I never forget how fortunate I was to get you, Emilie.'

She examined the mirror, then said, 'Who are your competitors? Names, please.'

A colleague in the staff room at school – Bertram, the English teacher – told me a sure-fire way of getting any wife to melt. 'Eat nothing, in the evening. You'll see how that impresses her. If you don't touch your evening meal, she'll realise you're lovesick. Leaving your food untouched on the plate is known, internationally, to be a sign of love.'

'I don't know, Bertram.'

'Just try. At night, when she's sleeping, you can always creep down and raid the fridge.'

'What do you think of his method, Kâzim? I can't tell by your expression. You only very rarely give your thoughts away, don't you? I imagined how Emilie would notice my lack of appetite, and ask, 'Lukas, dearest. I see you're not eating a single thing. Is something wrong?'

'Yes, Emilie, sweetheart,' I'd say in reply. 'It's nice of you to ask. You know, I'm yearning for you, but don't know whether perhaps you wish for something better. Are you still happy with me?'

She'd have no option but to melt. – Do you agree, Kâzim?

So, that evening, like a professional hunger artist, I passed on Emilie's fresh-from-the-garden seasonal salad, her unbeatable spinach savoury cake, and the caramel flan Markus had proudly helped her with, and how should I put it? The fact his caramel flan remained practically untouched offended him so much, he ran away from the table and cried beneath his bedcover like the twelve-year-old child he still was. When she looked over at me, Emilie's eyes were aflame.

'I love you, Lukas Zbinden,' she said.

I jumped, I got such a fright. When Emilie addressed me by my full name, I'd reason, normally, to tremble.

'And,' she continued, 'you should do everything you can to retain this love.'

From that day onwards – 12th August 1967 – forty-seven-year-old Lukas Zbinden put his shoulder to the wheel. He lent a hand with all the housework: cooking;

washing; even scrubbing the floor. He rolled his sleeves up, put an apron on, and fussed around zealously while Emilie sat at the sewing machine, threw her head back and looked out of her workshop, unable to believe what she was seeing.

I kept a list and ordered the different tasks according to urgency. If Emilie asked me to run an errand, I gave this priority. Emilie was soon so convinced the method worked, she no longer bothered asking me to do certain things, but noted on my list herself what she wanted done.

If guests dropped by, I brewed coffee and passed sweet things round, and Emilie explained to the guests how the 'world' had suddenly 'turned upside down' in this household. For a while, nothing made me happier than managing to get the ring cake out of its mould in one piece.

It's said that, in a clearing in a forest, there are two deckchairs, reserved for the couple that has never – not for a moment – regretted meeting. To this day, the deckchairs have remained untaken. I mention this story at my grand-daughter's confirmation, with the different generations assembled around the last scraps of our buffet, and Emilie shouts across the hall to me, 'Our names are on those deck-chairs, Lukas!'

Couples whose marriage has lasted fifty years are asked every now and then for the secret of their success. And yet it's not a closely guarded secret. You know each other really well; know all your strengths and – especially – your weaknesses; you treat your partner with care and respect; you admire and forgive each other. Emilie and I were a couple who had occasion to forgive each other time and time again. I forgave Emilie for not being a town walker. And she forgave me for often getting it wrong when I gave her a present. The cashmere pullover I bought at Schaufelberger's was two sizes too small; the perfume bought at Loeb was too strong; and it was well known she'd never liked orchids, even if Ryffel had grown them themselves. She forgave me for putting the salad bowl back in the fridge with only a cherry tomato left in it, just to avoid the washing-up. Only once did we really quarrel. She'd gone on a glider pilot course, and not told me beforehand. – Of course, you may ask what we're doing here! After all, it's almost your sofa, Herr Imhof! How happy you must be! – An exceptionally comfortable sofa, of the highest . . . – But that's not what we're doing. We're on our way out, and just stopped for a breather. – You're making out we're vandals. And it's not as if we're leaving cigarette ash, or eggshells, or anything else, lying here. But we shouldn't, of course, have taken a seat here, you're quite right, Herr Imhof. Your sofa is to blame: it's the magical effect it has on me. It reminds me so much of the sofa on which my brother and I were breast-fed. – You don't believe me? – For three years now, I've been wishing it could be moved to the floor I'm on. – Fixed to the floor, you say? – Get up, please, Kâzim, – it's time we were moving on. Thank you, Herr Imhof, for not calling the police.

We'll not make that mistake again, Kâzim. Now we've escaped from that holy terror, I feel quite shaky. It was just really bad luck that he had to come by at that moment.

Herr Imhof is ill. His soul's rotting. I explained it to him. 'Herr Imhof,' I said, 'if you continue the way you're going, there will soon be a smell from your throat. Don't you realise your soul's rotting? When something rots, it ferments. If something ferments, vapours arise, poisonous gas rises into your head, and that's what gives you your headaches.'

I explain it to him, but he just goes into a rage. Throws a cushion at me.

'At the age of eighty-eight, one really shouldn't be throwing things around,' I say.

Seeing someone rotting away is the most pitiful, distressing thing imaginable.

What do you think, Kâzim, maybe it will just take a minor event, something unlikely, to get Herr Imhof and Frau Jacobs together again? Maybe Frau Jacobs just needs to get stuck in the lift?

Imagine the scene: Frau Jacobs pressing the alarm – and such is her grief and misery, she's wailing and hammering the lift door with her free hand.

'What's that?' Herr Imhof – on the second floor – asks, holding his hand to his ear.

'Lift No. 1 is stuck,' the caretaker explains.

'Judging by the voice, it's Frau Jacobs,' the head of administration says.

'What can we do to help?' Herr Imhof asks, concerned.

The caretaker shrugs his shoulders. 'The operator company is sending out a mechanic. We'll just have to wait.'

'Wait?' Herr Imhof cries. 'And what if the lovely Julia goes and suffocates on us?'

His face shows a determination of which no one would have thought him capable any more. The framed photo of the Home around 1920 has already been snatched from the wall, and the frame shoved into the bi-parting door, to prise it open. Major Imhof is back in the militia.

The head of administration opens her eyes and discovers in the inconspicuous resident of Room 303 a sprightly man with hidden talents.

'What are you doing?' she stammers.

Herr Imhof looks down the shaft to the cage, in which Frau Jacobs has spent the last fifteen minutes, straining her arthritic arm and learning to pray in a standing position.

'For goodness sake!' the head of administration shouts. Herr Imhof takes a firm hold of the elevator rope and slowly lowers himself down the lift shaft in the direction of Frau Jacobs.

The caretaker chooses this moment to alert the head of admin, now paralysed with fear, to the fact that something's not right in this Home: on numerous occasions already, he's found empty wine bottles in the kitchen storeroom.

Smoking is forbidden in the lift, and Herr Imhof makes an unfriendly remark regarding the 'diktat of the

Management', as he calls it. Frau Jacobs, despite the awful situation she's in, manages to smile a little.

'I'm so afraid,' she says, embarrassed, and discreetly wiping the sweat from her brow.

'They'll soon get us out again.' Herr Imhof says, the *implicite* being: she needn't be afraid, he'll look after her. While abseiling down, he's lost a shoe, lacquered himself in grease from head to toe, and cut his index finger.

'Oh – you're bleeding!' Frau Jacobs says.

Herr Imhof hints that pain doesn't bother him. Today's the day for which he waited in vain back in the army.

To distract herself, Frau Jacobs tells him about the formal supper she attended at the home of acquaintances last night. Herr Imhof listens, interested, then asks, 'What were you wearing?'

Frau Jacobs has to fight back the tears. 'Do you know,' she reported to Lydia later, 'how long it's been since anyone asked me what I was wearing?'

The damaged door on the second floor delays the Schindler mechanic's rescue attempts by thirty minutes. Once Lift No. 1 is roadworthy again, and Frau Jacobs and Herr Imhof walk out of the cage, everyone – all those with hands to clap, and vocal chords up to cheering – acclaims them, from the head of administration to the new arrival on the fourth floor; from sociable walker Zbinden to lone wolf Ziegler. Tender arms are thrown round Herr Imhof's neck – and he faints.

'Loss of blood,' Britta and Lydia surmise, bedding the veteran down on a lounger. And a few months later, the entire Home assembles outside St Peter's on Kalcheggweg.

Both nearly ninety, Herr Imhof and Frau Imhof-Jacobs are, so Lukas Zbinden holds off until the last possible moment before buying them a wedding gift.

But I hope in vain. All that happens, and will continue to happen, is that Frau Jacobs and Herr Imhof walk past each other, their eyes fixed on something else. In the Dining Room, they ignore each other, dramatically. Frau Jacobs puts on her reading glasses and memorises the list of main courses, while Herr Imhof entertains the table with his tales of air combat in the clouds over England, such that you have to feel ashamed with – what's-her-name-again? – around. The intern. An Asian name. It's refusing to come to me.

That people are so lonely. And yet they're all living on top of each other, as never before. Do you hear people complain, Kâzim? A pupil says to me, 'No one bothers about me, no one treasures me, no one notices me. Not a single person loves me!'

I reply, 'Don't speak nonsense. Your parents love you.'

'What – them? A fight is all it'll take, and I'm off.'

'And your friends?'

'They're colleagues, no more than that.'

It's not just young people that can suffer this kind of loneliness, would you agree? Orphaned grammar-school pupils, alone in bed with a comic. A husband and wife can live together, and be desperately lonely, alongside each other. The husband has no idea what moves his wife. The wife has no idea what moves her husband. And then the dams burst. The husband who merely exists alongside his wife starts collecting Personal Development certificates. The fifteen-year-old with frightened eyes seeks comfort in a holiday job. Am I right? The spirits punish us humans if we don't keep up with all the many things we have to do. And if we do keep up, they punish us for not giving ourselves more to do. Men die early, don't live long enough to see the birth of their children's children.

And behind all this fussing: a distress that knows no bounds. Even the hours we have for ourselves should be spent productively, they say. It's absolutely not the case that everyone who moans about too much work getting to him feels better if the work *stops* getting to him.

The manager of the Home sits down with a sigh, and says, 'Oh, if only I could switch the phone off! It never stops: people are always wanting things from me.'

Frau Wyttenbach says, 'Be glad your phone still rings occasionally. I'd be happy if mine did. Have you come to a decision regarding the Gandhi matter?'

'If I feel like seeing Stefanie, it's Christine who comes,' Frau Rieter says, 'and if I feel like seeing Christine, Stefanie comes.'

'No one's interested in my opinion any more,' Herr Probst says. 'At first, I thought it would be wonderful to have peace for once, and to pass on all responsibility for business matters. Now, though, if I visit the firm, someone offers me a drink, and that's it. I might just as well not bother.'

'Never a free moment,' the manager says, getting up

with a sigh. Truly a rising star in the world of care for the elderly.

Before they went out to hunt, cave dwellers would draw images of antelopes and bears on the walls – to lure the animals. Am I speaking to you, Kâzim, to lure my family here? And yet I shouldn't complain. Other elderly people here grow lonely because they've no relations and are all on their own, or because their very busy children as good as never drop by. Frau Felber has grandchildren of every age between minus-three-months and twenty-four. Do you know what she has to do to 'see' them, though? She goes up to the attic and looks across the roofs until she spots the buildings she reckons they live in. To cheer her up, I sometimes join Frau Felber when she hunts for bargains at the half-price rails, in boutiques. She no longer thinks to buy presents for others, just herself. I've encouraged the Management here to send written warnings to anyone who doesn't visit their parents once a fortnight, at least.

Do you hear the people, Kâzim? 'I'm so lonely. No one gives me their love.'

I can't listen to them. 'And you?' I say. 'Show me the person who will announce: I'll give people my love!'

When the typist arrives at the beginning of her fixed hours – just to give you an example – Herr Hügli is usually outside the office already, waiting to look through the previous day's scrap. He robs the envelopes of the stamps, to send to his semi-baked great-grandchildren.

Or take Frau Dürig. Her three-year-old great-grand-children cuddle up as close as possible to her, lay their heads on her scrawny chest, and tell her stories that, with her twenty-per-cent hearing, she can barely follow. But while her great-grandchildren are speaking, she pets them and hugs them as tenderly as she once hugged her beloved husband. On one occasion, when I spoke to her about it, she said, 'Yes, Tobias and Noah remind me of my husband. I feel especially close to him when the children are with me.'

Have I already mentioned my grandfather to you, Kâzim? The key to many things that were to happen to me. He'd charge up to my brother and me, put his arms round our waists, and lift us, both at once. We'd kick our legs in the air, our clogs would clatter to the ground. He'd put us down again, hold his hand out, boom, 'Give me twenty!' and start to guffaw.

When Rudolf Minger was elected to government and welcomed back to Schüpfen – where he was living at the time – with drums beating and trumpets sounding, Mat-thäus and I really wanted to be there to see it. Grandfather laughed at us. 'Why do you want to see him, old farmer that he is?'

'But he's now a Federal Councillor,' Matthäus fought back.

Grandfather guffawed again. 'What are you thinking? Do you think Federal Councillors are special or what? That they can put their trousers on without putting first one leg in, then the other, like everyone else?'

'He's helping the poor!'

'Oh, Matthäus,' – but on the day Minger was welcomed back, Grandfather was waiting for us on the village's main street. Balloons. Garlands. An ox on the spit. We thought we'd arrived early, but the crowd was so large already, it looked as if we'd get nowhere near the station. Matthäus and I could have sat down and cried.

Except: Grandfather, with his brown bowler that made him look so suave, wasn't put off so easily. 'Both of you take my hands, and stay close at all times.' Then – with a loud, official-sounding voice – he started shouting, 'Step aside, please! *Please* make way!'

The people really did step aside and let us through. When we reached the station, Grandfather headed straight for the first policeman he saw. The tone he spoke in made him sound as if he were, at the very least, an artillery major. 'These two lads are Dr Duvalier-Delacroix's sons. Dr Duvalier-Delacroix is part of the entourage of Federal Councillor Minger. We need to get to the platform!'

That's torn it, I thought, but the policeman pushed his way through the crowd ahead of us, shouting repeatedly, 'Step to the side, please! Out of the way!'

He escorted us right up to the platform, where a brass band and women in traditional costume and men in their Sunday best were awaiting the Federal Councillor. The policeman pointed to a white mark on the ground. 'That, roughly, is where Minger's car will stop.'

'May I have your name?' Grandfather asked.

'Raaflaub,' the policeman said. 'Constable Raaflaub.'

'Thank you, Constable Raaflaub,' Grandfather said, lifting Matthäus and me onto his shoulders. 'I won't forget you.'

I reckon no other children inhaled the tobacco smoke from so close up as my brother and I did when the train finally arrived, Federal Councillor Minger got out of the first-class compartment, cheroot between his lips, and – before he turned to the crowd, beaming and waving – nodded to his wife that he wanted to keep the ticket collector's copy of the railway timetable until such time as the latter paid him the nineteen francs he'd lost to him, fair and square, in the card game they'd played between Berne and Schüpfen.

Believe it or not, Kâzim, I hate annoying people – other than my son – with speeches. But I can get angry sometimes and ask, 'What the hell do you give life? Day in, day out, you help yourself to the earth, the air, the beauty of this world. – And what do you give back?'

One day, Grandfather tells us to follow him. He's wearing a black suit and the brown bowler, and has a sophisticated walking stick with a silver handle. Side by side, we do his usual walk. First, down to the pond, where Matthäus and I are up to our necks in water, and churn up the mud at the bottom with both feet until Grandfather pulls us out, telling us stories about boys who drowned here. It's along the cool forest path next and, finally, through the gloomy quarry. We tell him about the pranks we've played, how the Tour de Suisse is going, the highs and lows of life in our Scout Group, and hang on Grandfather's every word as he tells us about the adventures of David Livingstone in Africa and Dr Barnardo's work among the children in the slums of

London. We reach a clearing near Grächwil and Grandfather explains, 'Here, they'll soon be erecting electric pylons.'

We've taken our shoes off and are carrying them, tied together, over our shoulders. When we reach Grächwil, Grandfather stops at a mound overgrown with grass, looks at it for a long time and says, 'The men doing army refresher courses used to have their firing range here.' He blinks at us, quickly, from the side. 'My pupils occasionally dig up bullets.'

'I want to be just like you when I grow up,' my brother says. 'I want to be a teacher.'

And with a cheerful voice, Grandfather replies, 'Being a teacher isn't a profession. It's a cross to bear. If you really want to be a teacher, train first to be an animal tamer. Maybe, with enough willpower and mastery of the art of seduction, you'll succeed in making a herd out of a horde.'

On the way back, Grandfather spots the sorry state of our shoes and takes a banknote from his wallet that he puts in Matthäus' hand. 'I want you to buy proper shoes with that.'

And before we can object, he shouts, 'Right now!' and we rush into the Agricultural Cooperative and buy high black shoes that get stone-hard when it's wet.

Who is it that drives you to become interested in the things that, one day, really interest you, Kâzim? Rudolf Minger's memorial, in Schüpfen, is a plain concrete wall, with cows grazing beside it. My grandfather's tomb is decorated with hydrangea and geraniums, and there have been no weeds in the pots – ever – for five decades now.

•

Isn't it odd – I know, for example, as good as nothing about the experiences my son had with his grandparents, about his childhood and youth, when I wasn't there. There is a great silence between us.

When Markus turned twenty, we went on holiday as a family for the last time. Ibiza: warmth, sun and the cheap *peseta*. Emilie went to bed early, and in the Bagatelle, a night club decked out with bamboo and fishing nets, Markus hugged two slightly perspiring blondes called Pam. Our *Fonda* at the pier had a back entrance that was open all night. Markus and I got to test how sober we were when we climbed the steep stairs to our rooms.

'Being a father is one of the nicest things in life,' I raved, on the staircase. 'The miracle of it never ceases for me – seeing how you've changed from a helpless infant into a strong man who can turn the heads of English girls. It's staggering.'

'Mm,' he replied.

'What do you mean, "mm"?'

'Nothing.'

'What do you mean, "nothing"?'

In the morning, the steamer from the mainland was due. Emilie and I watched the preparations for it as Markus slept off his hangover. An old man was sweeping the harbour with a broom. A dog fell into the water. We were sitting in a harbour café. Around us: mothers with daughters wearing ribbons; priests; officers in pyjamas; skinny hung-over models; and local hippies waiting for money.

'We should, at some point, have proper conversations!'

'What do you want to speak to Markus about?' asked Emilie.

Late in the afternoon – Markus was still horizontal – Emilie and I walked into the centre of the island, to look at the sea one last time. Larks rose, a cuckoo called, bright green lizards raced from stone to stone. Old women were sitting in the field, watching the pig or family goat. Girls with straw hats hung their babies up in a tree and started scything the grass. We had something to eat in a village – bread and fried eggs – and when we were finished, the man who had served us helped Emilie put her rucksack back on. 'Why are you walking?' he asked. 'Are you German?'

'No.'

'So why then?' he repeated, uncomprehending.

In the red light of the evening sun, we left the village to find a place to sleep. We found a grove and started to unpack among the bushes. The air was heavy with the scent of thyme. We rolled ourselves up in our sleeping bags and chatted to the night-time sounds of the frogs, crickets, mosquitoes, donkeys, dogs and nightingales.

'There's this yearning simply to be with him,' I said, bitterly. 'This odd looking forward to something you know, something familiar, and then the disappointment when we *are* together. Because we can't speak to each other.'

'Do you remember?' Emilie asked. 'At tea, once, Markus said – he was eleven at the time, maybe – "Mama, you left a piece of cauliflower earlier." He was playing the strict father and tried to take my dessert from me. You sent him back to his seat, though. "Sit down, Markus," you said. "You should take more exercise, you're getting a crooked back."' Emilie laughed, with pleasure. 'You fought about anything and everything. But I reckon neither of you knows what about.'

'What was it about then?'

'It was always very flattering when my husband and my son competed for my attention.'

I want to tell you something quite openly, Kâzim: ever since Emilie's beautiful, kind eyes closed for the last time, I don't know what I can still take seriously. How can an elderly man oppose the fleeting nature of the universe? Finance anarchist groups? Invest in adopting children? Distribute Chinese plants that help against rheumatism? Sell plots at the deserted edges of towns and hope in the name of the heirs for a building boom? I miss our daily little tendernesses: touching her hair as we pass; kissing her neck as she folds the washing; her hand on my thigh as we listen to classical music requests.

Very suddenly, Emilie was always tired. Everything was a strain for her, and she seemed to catch every infection going, every single infection from far and wide. Our GP gave her a blood test, and both he and the specialist to whom she was referred suggested a bone marrow biopsy to get a clear picture of her illness. She was assured such examinations were quite harmless. But she'd heard of a few people who had found them very painful and, certainly, very unpleasant. She knew that if you embark on such tests, you get tied up with a series of doctor and hospital appointments, and she didn't have the least intention of spending the little time remaining to her waiting in hospital departments. What's more, we had enquired and learned that the treatments suggested when leukaemia is diagnosed can at best prolong life for a short period. Emilie declined the bone marrow biopsy. She was always convinced that *how long* you live isn't what counts. Nine months later, she died at home.

It was a long, protracted death. Her condition worsened, remained like that for a while, worsened again. Emilie became thinner and smaller, looked like a bird. I accompanied her to the toilet – had to lift her up and drag her. On one occasion, we fell. Emilie was lying on top of me. I couldn't move, and she didn't have the strength to push herself off, or turn away. Our son, who – mystifyingly – had set out on a whim to visit us that evening, helped me to get up and carry her to bed. The next day, we arranged a home assistance service.

'How long can you stay?' I asked Markus as we waited for the nurse.

'A week, for sure,' he said. 'Longer, if necessary.'

I was grateful, and also surprised, as I'd been convinced he'd have to think long and hard about how to rearrange his professional duties.

The nurse came in the mornings to attend to Emilie, to treat her wounds with ointments. She put a nappy on her, and clean clothes. I performed these tasks when the nurse wasn't there. I removed the used nappy, cleaned her, put ointment on the open sores, and put a clean nappy on. Emilie put up with this without complaining, but I knew what she was feeling as I attended to her. The fact she was creating dirt, that she stank, that she was causing so much work, troubled her. When I washed her, I talked to her, an attempt to distract her.

'Emilie, try hard and get well.'

She tried to meet my gaze, smiled almost imperceptibly.

'Please get well, Emilie.'

She looked at me. Emilie had beautiful, hazelnut-brown eyes – have I mentioned that already?

And imagine, Kâzim: she said, 'Lukas, what do *you* hold on to?'

At night I hardly slept: listening to her every breath, and jumping up immediately and sitting beside her if she made the slightest sound.

Markus bought vegetables, in rough amounts, and threw them together in the kitchen. Emilie ate only tiny morsels, but she ate with pleasure. She was pleased with the food, praised Markus, and asked even in the morning, 'What are we eating later? Are you cooking another fabulous stew, like yesterday?'

The nurse attended to Emilie professionally, and lovingly. She was skilled and fast. She showed me the most important handholds. How to lift Emilie, minimising the pain. It was just that I handled her emaciated, sore body so fearfully, I prolonged the torture. Even if the nurse did the work, it hurt Emilie, and my clumsy handholds were worse still. She tried to control herself, whimpered quietly, whispered, 'That hurts, dear,' and I needed all my strength not to collapse beneath her pain. I couldn't watch her lying in her own dirt – I *had* to hurt her. That was the worst part, believe me.

Bouts of pain tortured her, inexpressibly. She slept in between, or lay awake. We took turns at being with her – Markus, Verena and I. So someone was always there to hold her hand.

The last words Emilie spoke to me. We're alone in the bedroom. Emilie's sleeping peacefully, her face lit by the afternoon light. The light of painters. I'm exhausted but just thinking what a wonderful person Emilie is. How much joy we shared: she always had something incredible in store. Her life was full – incredibly full – of friendship and cheerfulness; she was always so buoyant, and grateful. With her, each day was a gift.

She opens her eyes. 'Lukas?' she asks, faintly.

'I'm here, Emilie.'

She turns her head to me and manages to whisper, with difficulty, 'Do you remember that crystal-clear lake we were at? You were trying to catch trout with your bare hands? Were up to your knees in the water.'

'You advised me to learn to swim. So as not to drown, if ever the water was deeper.'

'In Kandersteg, as we waited for the train, you stole a dark-red rose from a garden. You bit off the thorns and spat them out. You held the rose up to my face. Then said I should consider marrying you. If you'd not asked, I'd have asked you.'

She sees the tears on my cheeks, me shaking my head. Then closes her eyes. Without stopping to think what I'm doing, I get into the bed beside her and put my head beside hers on the pillow. Her hand feels for mine, and we lie there for half an hour maybe. Then she dies. Without a sigh. Without the slightest struggle.

Thus died the person I loved like nothing else. Losing Emilie was – but what am I saying? You know yourself what it is to lose someone, and if you don't, you will one day. I thought of all the things I wished I'd said to her; of all the things I wished I'd done. In the end, I knew only that we should appreciate each other more. We should all appreciate each other more, and show it before it's too late.

May the road rise to meet you – an amateur choir, in which Emilie had sung, performed that song at the funeral. Their farewell greeting. Never had the choir failed as on this occasion. No one could hit the notes, for sobbing. I can tell you one thing: if Emilie were still here with me, and I could make a wish, I know what it would be: to be allowed to die with her.

After her death, you see, Kâzim, I was just about crushed by the pain and loneliness. Devoured by longing for the person I missed. How was I supposed to live for a single moment without her? I broke out in cold sweats as I walked through the suddenly empty house. I tried hard to trust in God more, but I'm not very religious. After all, there isn't just one god:

all those galaxies of stars and everything – they *must* be gods, whole flocks of them.

The family's care for me was touching, as was the compassion of the many people wishing to express their sympathy. Flowers were sent to comfort me, but I missed Emilie terribly. It was ghastly to open the door, knowing that Emilie wasn't there to greet me, beaming with joy and wanting to hear all about my day. I became a complete stranger to myself when people phoned and asked, with the best of intentions, how I was – they'd known Emilie well.

'I don't remember you,' I'd say, with a tremble in my voice, and replace the receiver.

I couldn't bring myself to hang the wet washing up; to take the bin out; to cook. A single occasion excepted, when I roasted a tough chicken, and left it in the oven overnight. It disintegrated: a sticky black mass. The clay pot was done for. I can't find my thermal socks. What will I do with her sewing things? I can't find the door key – it was always Emilie who took her key out when we arrived back together. Why eat? Why put flowers in vases? I'm forced to play a role that doesn't suit me. I think unkind things like 'Good world, now try and get along without me.'

The family stood by me. We sat down to share out Emilie's jewellery. Markus, Verena, Angela and I. With each individual piece, we considered 'Who would that suit?'

Markus and I insisted on Verena getting a certain pair of earrings: we reckoned they were her style. And, together, Markus and I convinced Angela to accept a particular ring as, in our opinion, it suited her perfectly. At that moment, I felt as close to my son as rarely before.

But when I'm alone again, I just stare, in jaded fashion, at our bed, where she died; I stare into drawers; stare gloomily at her hairbrushes in the bathroom cabinet; and stare at envelopes addressed to her – a form of torture. Post kept on coming for her for such a long time.

It rains, and the rain hammers down on the flowers covering her grave, extinguishing the candles that surround it. I still have to have the gravestone erected. The neighbouring graves are already done. I don't know what kind of stone to choose. A woman lays flowers on a child's grave, some rows away. I cry and don't move. It would take an earthquake to move me. A volcanic eruption. Or a trick. A simple self-deception.

Do you remember how it was to be a child? You banged your head, and your mother kissed it better? I imagined Emilie kissing my pain better. Bending down and pressing her lips on my temple. And do you know what? Imagining that gave me strength. My voice brightened up. I felt almost protected. Protected in a way I hadn't felt for months. And then I asked myself what Emilie would have done, in my place. How *she* would have proceeded. What Emilie would have thought of staring into a drawer; at a grave.

No, she wouldn't have allowed a healthy, intelligent person to die of grief. Especially not if *she* was that person. Before giving up on herself, she'd have told herself to walk round the cemetery, thrice. She'd have done what needed doing, would've given herself a smack in order to wake up and face reality. She'd have mopped the floor, washed the dirty cloths out, cleaned the sink. She'd have gone to the potato growers' village, to visit a lifelong friend.

So I pulled myself together. The photo albums made their way into the cupboard. A carpet that had slipped a little was re-positioned. A bowl of dried flowers was placed on the table. The handles of the umbrellas in the copper stand were disentangled. Bills were put away, properly, in folders. I didn't go to the extreme of cleaning the windows, but I folded the dishcloths with a precision that even for an eighty-four-year-old bordered on pathological.

Then I left the house and asked Emilie to join me, as she'd always done. To walk beside me, in intimate togetherness: I know what you're feeling, you know what I'm feeling. – That's not supernatural, Kâzim! Not any more so than the telephone. The spirits are here, around us. We just lack the right apparatus.

On a whim, I started asking for things for other people. Two men laying a cable: I asked Emilie to give them a good wage. I saw a woman hanging out laundry: the long lines full of children's clothes told me she had a large family to care for. I asked Emilie to give her an untroubled life, a helpful husband and healthy children. At the bus stop, I saw a young man crouched beside the bench, dozing. I asked Emilie to have him wakened; and to give him the blessing of a varied job. Is there something wrong with me, Kâzim? Something age-related, maybe? I was *convinced* each request had immediate effect!

On the way home, I took the tram. I was sitting behind a woman who seemed depressed. I'd seen her face as I boarded the carriage and now asked Emilie to relieve her of her depression. At that moment, the woman reached for the back of her head, and when she got off a little later, the gloomy look had vanished from her face. There was a smile, even! I like to tell myself that Emilie often succeeds in improving the atmosphere in a tram.

Once, Markus was struggling, resentfully, to lift a heavy stone. He's a proud little boy. Emilie, watching, asks after a while, 'Tell me, are you really doing all you possibly can?'

'Of course. Can't you see that?'

'I don't believe you,' Emilie replies, 'because, so far, you haven't asked me to help you.'

He looks at his mother as if she were a magician.

You should know, Kâzim: my daughter-in-law lives in permanent fear of some unspecified, terrible thing that might happen. She's just waiting for some unhappy event to affect her, or her family. A runny nose, conjunctivitis, a corn – all grow, in her imagination, into something monstrous. She carefully avoids letting it show that it worries her if her daughter has a date on Saturday with a young Frenchman. But her feelings betray her when Angela comes home on Sunday and discovers that, for no reason her mother can voice, the latter is angry and irritated. Verena's worn-out look tells me she'd give a lot to be more relaxed. I'll ask Emilie to give her peace of mind. And let's see what happens.

•

– When? Three years ago in autumn. A stumble helped me to take the last seven rungs of the wretched ladder in a oner. I only broke a few minor bones, but the experience persuaded the family it was time to sit down and talk to me. 'Pensioner lay helpless by his bed for nine hours', they read aloud and told me about all the infirm elderly for whom no one comes when they cry for help. Verena confessed that it troubled her to think of me trying to struggle along all alone. I can still do everything myself, true, but I realise I'm not the youngest any more. At least, not as young as I was in my early eighties.

Before I moved here, to the town I grew up in, and where Markus and his family live, I ceremoniously watered the roses outside our house in Unterseen, and cut the withered shoots off.

'Have you ever thought about roses?' Emilie had asked once. 'They never hurry, don't get into a fret. They don't make any noise, or answer any phone calls. They just grow and bloom, and give us contentment.'

Emilie had caressed the rosebush every now and then, she loved it so much.

The first thing Verena's brother did, having hardly moved into our house, I heard, was pluck out all the herbs. He didn't know what they were. The plums and pears on the fruit trees, he left to the wasps. The walnut tree left the house too much in the shade, he claimed, which was why he wanted to decapitate it.

I remember the day I arrived here, chauffeured by Markus. He gave me a lecture about the damage martens can do to your car, and I was terribly downcast as I thought it would be hard living with so many people I didn't know. The bed, the lamps, the curtains, the stool, I brought with me. A few books with tattered covers; the photo albums; Emilie's pearl necklace; and three hand-woven cushions from our honeymoon in Provence, the colours now faded. A few records. To our great pleasure, we'd chanced upon this record shop in Arles where, for a small fee, we could sit and listen to operas all that rainy afternoon. I thought it better not to have too many reminders of things round about me.

The then manageress of the Home welcomed me to my room with a few friendly words, a bunch of flowers, information about the Home, and a flyer for a session called 'Gymnastics for the Over-80's'.

'We don't have a Care Department as such, but we strive to look after our residents here until their dying day,' the manageress said. 'When it comes to washing your own things, the Laundry Room – with its washing machines, airing cupboard and tumble-dryer – is at your disposal. At no extra charge, you can always have your washing done for you.'

The information included a list of classes on a huge variety of things. The contemplation of candles with the Prayer Group; light baths; memory training; reading newspapers; the Biography Group; 'Making Gifts with Irina'; How to use a Swiss ball – *we lift a ball above our heads and try to do knee bends to make sure we haven't stiffened up*. The classes were a good way of settling in, I was told, and to get to know the residents. 'Speaking of the residents, Herr Zbinden,' the manageress said, 'weren't you a teacher in your day? What subjects did you teach?'

'My favourites were Geography and German.'

'Might you like to offer a class on Swiss Geography, for those who are interested?' she asked. 'Or on handwriting?'

Given that my own handwriting's terrible, I regard it as the joke of my career that I once taught it. I said. 'No, if I take a class, then one on *walking*. If that's not on offer already.

'Good idea,' the manageress said, though she couldn't possibly know what it would entail.

And so, in my first weeks in the Home, I immersed myself, principally, in the preparation of my class on walking. I wanted the class to be refreshing and exhilarating, and at the same time to have a moral impact, concealed – of course – beneath a cheerful surface, as people generally don't like listening to moralising. I came across possible participants in the Dining Room; or on the leather armchairs in the Day Room, their legs crossed and stretched out before them as they tapped with their favourite gloves. I sat alone at an empty table in the Dining Room and just stared at my tray with its polenta, beans and pudding. Or sat down, bravely, with my tray in front of me, beside a trio of tame-looking ladies who were bending over their food so absentmindedly, they could have been astral-travelling between bites. Once, when I sat down beside Herr Wenk, he said, with his mouth full and typically tersely, 'That seat's taken.'

I imagined how I'd begin the course: 'Ladies and

Gentlemen, my roots lie back in time immemorial when the world was not yet a village, but a sphere. I'll be friendly to you, and I want you to be friendly to me. I'm offering a series of classes on walking, as I am afraid of your dying jaded.'

I'd be taking the reduced retentiveness of senior citizens into consideration. Those who didn't speak up in the theory lesson wouldn't be called on to answer questions. I would not be setting homework. Everyone would have the right to walk around freely or – if close to suffocating, the sweat pouring off them – to open or close the window. In the event of any tests in the practical part, limited used of public transport would be permitted.

With a furrowed brow and evident difficulty, Markus fought his way through the first pages of my lecture – and postponed further reading of it to his next visit, when he would have more time and peace for that kind of thing.

'It could be full of fascinating insights, things that are worth knowing,' I said, to encourage him.

Markus looked at the pages, then at me, then back at the pages. 'Rain walkers have become accustomed to regarding the rain that's teeming down on them positively,' he quoted. 'After all, the best thing you can do when it's raining is just let it rain.' He got up. 'Thanks a lot, hey.' Trembling with impatience, he added, 'I have to go. The parking meter's running out.' In one hand, he was holding my manuscript out to me. In the other, my medicine.

'Back then,' I said, 'I kept vigil over Emilie. The whole night long. She couldn't decide whether she was in labour or not. When the time came, I was blissfully asleep.'

Markus laughed. 'I attended preparation courses for weeks: how to make giving birth painless. And when the time came, I was flat out: in a dead faint on the floor. Neither of us passed the first test of fatherhood with flying colours, exactly. Bye, Dad.'

He stopped at the door, turned around again. 'All the best for the class,' he said, tenderly, 'and take care.'

I don't know, Kâzim, I'm discovering new traits in my son. And I ask myself: did I overlook them before? Or has he become more open to me with age?

Being a father was never easy for me – never as easy as being a walker, a teacher, Emilie's husband, a resident, here in the Home. Lukas Zbinden, who – without blinking an eye – would call himself the last of the meek, isn't happy with a whole host of things as regards his relationship with his son. I know I can no longer solve any major problems. And believe me, that weighs twice as heavily when it's to do with my own son. It would be good if we were to use the time we'll still share.

And indeed: four weeks after I moved into the Home, the manageress chased a group of slightly confused souls out into the courtyard, where they looked around, irritated. She told the group where to sit, on the folding chairs set out beneath the chestnut tree, where there was enough shade to spend a fair amount of time. A balmy autumn afternoon. The manageress apologised to me as she'd have to leave my lecture after fifteen minutes, owing to other commitments elsewhere. She then closed the glass door back into the Home and leaned against it, gripping the handle tightly. She gave me a signal. Sitting on the stone bench beside the fountain, I began to lecture. I was simultaneously excited and calm. Felt a little like a singer who, after what was supposed to be his last performance ever, returns to the stage.

'Ladies and Gentlemen, have you ever felt afraid of your own jadedness? Either you're not jaded; or the fact that you *are* protects you from a fear of the same. Anyone with the slightest respect for himself and his senses can grasp that there's nothing worse than a jaded life, i.e. one without feeling. If we learn to fear this dullness, we'll ask: where's the way out of this? And we'll realise: walking is the way out. Every step can become a walk.'

It all seemed to be going smoothly until Herr Imhof, in the first row, realised what had happened to him: he'd been dragged to a lecture that didn't in the least interest him. What he wanted was to lean out of his window and observe the street below. Instead, sheer bad luck had led him, on his way back from a piece of home-made Black Forest Gateau in the Cafeteria, to bump into the manageress. He'd had no intention whatsoever of listening to my Jaded-Fog Speech in a moderately busy courtyard that got very little sun, when there was all that lively activity out on the street. He stood up and, walking sideways, made a quick exit. Instantly, three others who'd been dragged along seized the chance to flee. Messrs Wenk and Hügli, and Frau Steinimann, who died last spring. They rushed past the manageress and – making sufficient noise for me to be forced to lower my papers and pause – fled indoors, back to artificial light.

Geriatric Nurse Britta took advantage of this disturbance. 'When does the Laundry close today?' she asked Lydia.

'Four.'

'Damn,' Britta said, struggling to her feet. 'Come on, Lydia.'

Lydia had just slipped her shoes from her swollen feet and found a comfy position. She looked overworked and exhausted and seemed not to mind this chance to snooze beneath the chestnut before having to rush to Frau Jacobs with the pipette. Now, she was reluctantly following Britta to the Laundry. This seemed to encourage the entire left wing: they stood up as one and got in under the roof. Frau Schaad, not yet paralysed down one side at that point, turned her head in surprise and, fearing she might miss her chance, rushed after those hurrying off. Her folding chair fell over with a bang.

Five people remained. Herr Ruchti, Madame Revaz, Frau Dürig, the then civilian-service carer, Sebastian, and the manageress. I gathered my papers together and encouraged them to leave too. Maybe we'll meet on a walk some time, I murmured.

'I've got time,' Herr Ruchti said, smiling mildly. 'Feel free to continue to appeal a little to our consciences.'

Madame Revaz fished her glasses from her bag and asked would I mind if she knitted while listening. And

Frau Dürig said: at least it was more comfortable sitting here than in the Day Room, where it smelled of poor ventilation.

'Does life have a deeper meaning?' I continued, in spirited fashion. 'Is it a complete coincidence that we were born? I have a friend, a retired teacher. He was once invited to the home of an industrialist in Schlieren. The man, who was divorced from his wife three times, and went back to her three times, has a wonderful villa by the River Limmat. A hundred guests are romping around. The different sections of the shelves on the wall are filled with all kinds of decanters, vases, arty spice and herb containers. My friend meets the master of the house and says: You've got it good. You live like a king! A house like this! A profitable glass factory! A delightful wife! Dear children! And the man answers: Yes, you're right, things are going well for me. But, suddenly, he becomes deadly serious and says: But don't ask what it looks like in here, and he points to his heart.

The most important things, we should do first. And if walking frees us from melancholy, jadedness, lethargy, apathy, then the most important thing is that we go for walks.

People like to be outside in the fresh air. They rustle up open-air experiences for themselves: the nice view, for instance, that rewards the discomfort felt in the ears by cable car users. But the world is a hidden world; do you know what I mean when I say that? I'll explain, using an image: a thick wall of fog. Hidden behind the wall of fog is a rose. Now, people can't live without the rose. And so start to look for it. They throw footballs against the wall of fog, they hold playing cards, they attend evening classes, they form rows of four and play wind instruments in the orchestra. Those are the efforts involved in various leisure activities. The walker puts one foot in front of the other and penetrates the wall of fog. He finds the rose. A whole rose bush. Diminutive birds build their nest in its branches. Bugs nibble at its stem. He who finds the rose has found the world.

I often ask myself why people aren't bright and attentive. They're well off, for the most part, after all. But they can't be bright and attentive. Why? Because they're jaded. Asleep, completely drunk, indifferent. And no self-help book or teacher of a walking class is going to take away that feeling of jadedness. Only walking can do this. An encounter that inspires him, or seeing something that touches him, catapults the walker into a condition full of love, clear-sightedness and fulfilment. For as long, at least, as it takes him to return to the drab, joyless, everyday consciousness that most people have accepted as normal since they were taught as children always to close doors.

Why do we close doors? Even the door to the Dining Room is locked during meals. Not a breath of wind moving the white curtains. What is it we have to protect ourselves from so relentlessly? Wherever my late wife now is: there, the doors, for sure, aren't locked. So the wind can pass through the apartment, and who knows, maybe the doors don't even have locks: maybe it's only a string of beads that separates her apartment form the world outside it.

Listen: one of the beauties of this town is the green river that, as the poet says, *embraces the town*. I often go for a walk there. People jump in, to float from one bank to the other. Boats wherever you look, their sterns blunted. At the weir, a bridge leads across. The water crashes down the weir. And one day I see that where the water crashes down, a large piece of wood is dancing. I observe how the wood goes under and comes back up and turns in a circle. From time to time, it looks as if the current could come and carry it off. But the maelstrom grabs it again. When I return the next day, the piece of wood is still there. The vortex keeps getting hold of it. Can you imagine that? The current is there, and the wood comes up and goes under and turns in a circle. Human lives are often no different. It's always the same three windows that the world is seen through: the window in the room, the windscreen in the car, the goggle box. On the one hand, people know they need to act, if they want to change anything. On the other, that's exactly what they don't do, as they're afraid of the consequences. They ponder their discontentment, but in order not to have to act, they silence any unsettling thoughts with reassurances: It was a wonderful day, anyway, and I can't take too much sun. On the weir, I thought: all it would take is a push or a prod and the wood would enter the current. But I couldn't reach because I, a non-swimmer, didn't want to risk falling in. I swim like an anvil. Once, I fell into the learners' pool. All I heard was terrible gurgles, and bubbles rose to the surface.

Ladies and Gentlemen, we are not a piece of wood. The one step out of the only-ever-the-same circle, the one step into the current, is a step we ourselves can take. Do feelings sometimes threaten to overwhelm you? Do situations sometimes seem to be over your head? Does the whole world weigh on your weak shoulders? Are you unable to sleep out of sheer longing for your deceased husband? Do you not know how to show your son you love him? Then put one foot in front of another on the immaculately cemented-over bed of a stream, or in a biotope that is significant in terms of natural history. That is always possible, even when nothing else is. Ladies and Gentlemen, this walking course will help you open up your heart, such that your life will make sense, as in: become sensuous. Sensuousness is what makes sense possible, in the first place. You want facts, not a sermon. Walking means: going for a walk. Not, listening to lectures about walking. As the speaker, I feel like someone standing in front of a fountain, selling water. You've heard now what I have to say. You can think you've been taught something, or been re-orientated, or born again, or whatever you like. Believe me when I say that in the lives of sprightly people, walking plays at least as central a role as their profession, poetry, godparenthood, family and health. Thank you for your attention.'

The applause from my five listeners, at the end of the lecture, sounded friendly. Even if I could assess only with difficulty how *loud* it actually was – as my pupils, in the past, would only applaud if I distorted the word 'mashed potatoes' in twenty-three ways, something that had them howling with laughter. Today's pupils, I suspect, would shoot me down for fun like that.

'Good,' said Sebastian, helping Madame Revaz up from her folding chair, 'I'll contradict you for the duration of my stint here.'

A sceptical young man. Scared to death, he was, of catching a fatal disease here. On his first day as a civvy, he took a deep breath before entering the Home, then didn't breathe again for three months.

Herr Ruchti, at least, stretched his limbs and happily paid me several compliments that I played down, coolly. He said he rejected most of my views, and considered them alarming in almost every respect except, perhaps, with regard to their harmlessness. It had been exceedingly pleasant for him, though, to hear views so very far from his own. These words prompted the manageress and Frau Dürig to repeat Herr Ruchti's compliments, and once they were suitably enthusiastic, I accepted them. Let the devil take me if that's not Herr Pfammatter coming towards us. Look! I've told you about our folklorist, haven't I?

Good evening, Herr Pfammatter! Why, don't you always turn up just as we think we've heard the last of you! – Oh, dear, what do you look like? – No, no. Matted and damp. As if you were on your way back from an uncomfortable night in a cave – where you had had to hide from something, in the darkness, that you actually wanted to hunt. – Budapest, exactly! – Did you get a decent haul of souvenirs? – Let's see! – That's a lady's watch! How did you get your hands on a lady's watch? – At supper, whatever you think. Herr Probst wants to know whether you'd be available for a game later? – Pardon? – Kâzim, our new carer. A rower. A good listener. And a splendid escort. I must be as heavy as lead on his arm, but if I am, he doesn't let on. – No? What *would* you like to be praised for then, Kâzim? – Tomorrow, when you've recovered a little, Kâzim could visit you in your room and see the frightening collection of found items you have, what do you think, Herr Pfammatter? – Yes, no rush, just take your time getting changed, and see you later!'

Of course, we saw the talks on walking through – what did you think? The second lesson had to be postponed due to operations on Madame Revaz's eyes, but we then tested our skills out together – in the pretty courtyard, and on the street outside, beneath Herr Imhof's suspicious looks. Herr Ruchti, a yellow scarf wrapped round his neck, trudged three steps ahead of the others, his head back, and with a chortling laugh, setting the pace and determining the direction, very much the centre of this old-timers' expedition, while Herr and Frau Dürig talked enthusiastically about when they first met. Sebastian was wearing sunglasses even if the sun had no intention of breaking out from behind the cloud cover. They then sat – Madame Revaz, Sebastian, Herr Ruchti and the Dürigs in bizarre cuddly slippers – squeezed up together on the sofa that's been in the Day Room for generations.

Madame Revaz's feet were resting on a footstool with a knitted cover, the exact copy of the knitting in her hands.

They'd listen to what I had to say about proper walks, or look far back to their own early experiences as pedestrians, on the way to school and on forays, remembering injured and rescued animals, exploring building sites, finding bones in the forest, snowball fights.

'Once, in winter,' Herr Ruchti told us, 'I asked my father if I could take the horse to school as it was such a long way. Father said: okay then. We harnessed Sambo, hitched him up to the sleigh, Father walked alongside the horse. When we reached the summit and looked down on the village, it started to snow.'

You missed Herr Ruchti, Kâzim. A charming, white-haired beanpole, who – despite the classroom atmosphere in the Day Room – could amuse himself royally. He'd begin by chuckling secretly to himself, then burst out laughing, and regularly break into applause. As a teacher, you try hard not to have favourites, but Herr Ruchti, with his beaming smile, was my favourite participant on the course.

Madame Revaz would knit, Herr and Frau Dürig would doze off hand in hand, and Sebastian, always in tight T-shirts, as if he'd been pumped into them, would draw my attention to any contradictions. On his last day as helper, Madame Revaz opened her handbag and took out a scarf she'd finished knitting, of the finest black wool.

'For you, Sebastian,' she said and, touched, he wrapped the scarf around his bull neck. He then shook my hand till it was numb, and claimed he'd really enjoyed our 'slow-motion walks' though he didn't plan spending any more of his time on them. 'Maybe I enjoyed listening to you so much because every word you said confirmed, for me, that I haven't been missing much.'

In his face, I could see dozens of former pupils of mine.

I can well understand that Frau Dürig, for example, prefers to go for a walk with an understanding older person than with a twenty-year-old carer: it's the generation you know, you don't have to explain or apologise so much. But the fact I've contact here with you civilian-service boys, I consider an incredible stroke of luck. You hear so often that you should try to have young friends. I'm all the more thankful that young men like you, Kâzim, and Sebastian, are gifted to me. You haven't waited until you have to visit your own mother in a care home to discover solidarity with the elderly. For that, I thank you more than I can express in words.

What are you saying, Kâzim? The final step! Safely and fearlessly we've reached the ground floor! Boy, boy, – eighty-seven, but you're still making the likes of this look easy, Lukas Zbinden. Madame Revaz! Here we are, over here! – We've just been speaking about you. How are you? – What's your children's news? – Your daughter went to university, remember? – The boy has emigrated to Paraguay, married a nurse. You have good children, Madame Revaz, you should be proud of them! – Why, yes! – Do you maybe remember *when* you got married? – Of course, it's a long time ago! But when exactly? – You were born in 1919, weren't you? – Do you remember how old you were when you married? – Did you get married at twenty? No? – But you weren't thirty by the time . . . right? – Twenty-one maybe? – Twenty-two? – Could be. If you were twenty-three, you got married in 1942. Does that seem about right? 1942: marriage to Bértrand Revaz in the Eglise du Saint-Esprit in Delémont? – Let's return to the subject tomorrow, Madame Revaz. Think hard until then about when exactly you married. – Don't mention it! To the front door, Kâzim.

Nowadays, Madame Revaz can no longer knit. She listens to the TV, and is forgetting her past. How long, do you think, can we depend on ourselves? On our senses? On our minds? For how much longer will I wake in the morning with the memories I took to bed the evening before?

Once, Emilie and I were lying on a freshly mown meadow, watching the evening.

'*Happiness*,' I said to Emilie, 'what do you think of when you hear that word?'

'Can't you just enjoy the evening, quietly?'

'No, tell me.'

'Okay,' said Emilie, scratching her leg where a mosquito bite was annoying her. 'There is big and little happiness. Big happiness is our love. The little one would be if you'd just listen to the silence.'

Frau Schild, wait! – Just hand me the envelope. You don't need to put it in my pigeonhole. It's much more practical this way. – What's in it then? Increasing the flat rate for the running costs, are we, hm? – Pardon? – Alessandra?

She was turning the third floor upside down, trying to find Frau Binggeli's crown. – And Frau Jacobs is digging with her index finger inside her collar, to get at something itchy. Perhaps you could ask Lydia or Britta – or is Britta already on maternity leave? – I know nothing about that. Kâzim, did Herr Ziegler mention wanting to visit his wife? As far as I know, he just went up to his room to peel himself out of a garment. Is that your phone ringing? – Pleasure. It's not as if it's of any interest to us.

In four weeks, Nurse Britta will have a child. She's getting into a panic because the office at home is still an office and not a nursery.

Just a little spurt across the hall now and we can breathe again, after holding our breath for much too long. – What? – No, you won't get me into a wheelchair. – No, Angela pushed me around the squeaky corridor once, then – before I could protest – squeezed me out the door and into the street. She worked up quite a speed, I was rattled around like a sack of potatoes, she turned the corner and then, just as Brunnadernstrasse starts to climb slightly, she ran out of strength. I told you, I know, that I can't imagine a single trait my son has inherited from me. But Angela says, with a mischievous smile, 'I always tell Dad that he talks the head off Mum the exact same way he says you always talked Emilie's head off.'

You see, Kâzim: the shaggy carpet curls and blocks the entrance.

●

You can let go of my arm now, Kâzim. Thank you very much. Wind force zero. No butterfly's going to be thrown off course. But you can never know. This is precisely the type of weather that often has a storm in tow. And then the gullies overflow, the water washes the Parliament away, and politicians hit on the idea of abandoning politics and working instead – though not a single case occurs to me, that ended so badly. – Of course, the smoking ban's been reversed. Be my guest. As long as you don't throw the butt into the nettles. But I don't want to keep you any longer, have you considered it? Will you accompany me on a walk? – Really? – You mean, where? – To the river? Gladly! Do you have your boat nearby, by any chance?

I've told you about me, now it's your turn. – Oh, every-thing! How come you're here in the Home with us; how long you'll stay for; and whether you row in a club. A few remarks about human existence; about being a son; having a father. And, of course, whether you're married, engaged, or somebody's boyfriend. Who do you tell, in the even-ing, about what happened to you during the day? Do you celebrate religious feast days even when there's nothing to eat? Of the people you've contact with, which would only *you* subject yourself to, and no one else? You may also answer questions that haven't even been put to you. I do that, myself. Every day. – Possibly, but if I'm *curious*, then you're *stubborn*. Are we going to spend the entire evening here before the night-time bell? Fire away! – No, don't try to change the subject. I'm not budging from here until you start to spill some beans! Tell me some stories from different parts of your life! Or I'll go back in and dance in the lift naked, while the others try to escape as quick as they can. Then they'll put me in a home for the senile and I'll never be heard of ever again. – Pardon? – How to go for a proper walk? You want to know how to walk properly? Kâzim, were you listening to me *at all*, on the stairs? What are you even doing here at my side? I would say: if a goal has been reached and you haven't yet homed in on the next one, isn't there a gap there somewhere? – Now, extend that gap. That's going for a walk.

Oh dear, look over there: Gandhi, up in the chestnut. – No, I reckon, as long as he stays there, nothing can happen. He does, though, seem to be considering whether to jump over into Frau Wyttenbach's room. Was that a raindrop? – But please, to the river is wonderful! We could cross the footbridge and borrow a dinghy from the campers in Eichholz. I'll leave the rowing to you, if that's okay. I'd like to see you happy. Given you're already doing me the priceless favour of accompanying me! You're an angel, Kâzim!

He works away at it every Sunday. If the foot spar's not the problem, then it's the sliding seat, and if it's not the sliding seat, then it's the rowlock. I fear someone's fobbed some rubbishy rowing boat off on Kâzim. No, no, I didn't say I want to change him. You're putting words in my mouth again. Of course, he can continue to row! I just want not to have to race when in his company, and that's something quite different. At breakneck speed, we suddenly ran between parked cars out onto Brunnadernstrasse, which attracted semi-enraged, semi-worried looks from both the public and private transport using the road. I appealed to forgotten deities to give me some pace. More than once I was forced to say, 'Listen, Kâzim, we're not running, whether this dog chases after us or not.'

No, a big angry one. One that goes for any carer that looks it in the eye. – Emilie, listen. We finally shook off the dog in Elfenau, and I asked Kâzim could we stop to catch our breath. We were standing beside a phone box, and do you know what I thought? I thought: I could die, or lose my mind, without Markus and I having talked things out, and then I'd be terribly sorry. What are you waiting for, Lukas Zbinden? I roared at myself. Do you want to tell him what you feel for him only at the last minute? Don't try to fool yourself. What you don't talk about while in full command of your faculties, you're not going to talk about as a nursing case.

I summoned up all my courage and called our son. After I'd exchanged a few words with Verena, Markus came to the phone, and I said with my heart beating – I don't know what I was afraid of – 'I wanted to tell you I love you.'

There was silence at the other end, then the receiver was put down, and I could hear voices in the background. Our daughter-in-law came back to the phone and asked, concerned, 'What did you say to him?'

'I said I loved him – something I've never told him, and because I thought he'd maybe like to know.'

She said, 'Markus is sitting over there, fighting back the tears.'

And I reckon, maybe we still can go about things differently, different from before. We're not a piece of wood, right? That one step out of the always-the-same circle, that one step out into the current, we can take by ourselves.

Have you the feeling, too, that the whole house is gradually getting ready for supper? All that sniffing at the air, trying to guess what the main course is? You know, sometimes situations get too much for me. I'm so homesick for you, I can't sleep. At times like that, I just put one foot in front of the other and tell someone about you. Hold forth about your merits. Rave on about how complete life by your side is. That is always possible, even when nothing else is. Our names are, indeed, on those deckchairs, Emilie.

Dear readers,

We rely on subscriptions from people like you to tell these other stories – the types of stories most UK publishers would consider too risky to take on.

Our subscribers don't just make the books physically happen. They also help us approach booksellers, because we can demonstrate that our books already have readers and fans. And they give us the security to publish in line with our values, which are collaborative, imaginative and 'shamelessly literary' (the *Guardian*).

All of our subscribers:

- receive a first edition copy of every new book we publish
- are thanked by name in the books
- are warmly invited to contribute to our plans and choice of future books

BECOME A SUBSCRIBER, OR GIVE A SUBSCRIPTION TO A FRIEND

Visit andotherstories.org/subscribe to become part of an alternative approach to publishing.

Subscriptions are:

£20 for two books per year

£35 for four books per year

£50 for six books per year

The subscription includes postage to Europe, the US and Canada. If you're based anywhere else, we'll charge for postage separately.

OTHER WAYS TO GET INVOLVED

If you'd like to know about upcoming events and reading groups (our foreign-language reading groups help us choose books to publish, for example) you can:

- join the mailing list at: andotherstories.org/join-us
- follow us on twitter: @andothertweets
- join us on Facebook: And Other Stories

This book was made possible by everyone who subscribed to *Zbinden's Progress* before its first English-language publication in the UK. Thank you!

Our Subscribers

Adam Mars-Jones
Adrian Goodwin
Adrian May
Agnes Jaulent
Ajay Sharma
Alannah Hopkin
Alasdair Thomson
Alastair Dickson
Aldo Peternell
Alec Begley
Ali Smith
Alice Nightingale
Alison Hughes
Alison Layland
Alison Macdonald
Alison Winston
Amelia Ashton
Ana Amália Alves
Ana María Correa
Andrea Reinacher
Andrew Blackman
Andrew Marston
Andrew Tobler
Angela Thirlwell
Ann McAllister
Anna Athique
Anna Holmwood
Anna Milsom
Annalise Pippard
Anne Longmuir

Anne Meadows
Anne Withers
Anne Marie Jackson
Annette Nugent
Apollo Libri Kft

Bárbara Freitas
Barbara Glen
Barbara Latham
Barry Wouldham
Ben Thornton
Benjamin Morris
Brendan Franich
Briallen Hopper
Bruce Ackers
Bruce Holmes
Bruce Millar

Caroline Barron
Caroline Perry
Caroline Rigby
Catherine Mansfield
Cecilia Rossi
Charles Boyle
Charles Day
Charles Lambert
Charlotte Holtam
Charlotte Ryland
Charlotte Whittle
Charlotte Williams

Chloe Diski
Chris Stevenson
Chris Watson
Christina
    MacSweeney
Christopher Marlow
Ciara Breen
Ciara Ní Riain
Clare Bowerman
Clifford Posner
Colin Holmes
Constance and Jonty

Daniel Carpenter
Daniel Gallimore
Daniel Hahn
Daniel James Fraser
Dave Lander
David Attwooll
David Johnson-Davies
David Roberts
David Wardrop
Davida Murdoch
Debbie Pinfold
Deborah Bygrave
Deborah Smith
Deirdre Gage
Denis Stillewagt
Dominic Charles

Echo Collins
Eddie Dick
Eileen Buttle
Elaine Rassaby
Eleanor Maier
Emily Evans
Emma Kenneally
Emma McLean-Riggs
Eric Dickens
Erin Barnes

Fawzia Kane
Fiona Quinn

Gabrielle Morris
Gavin Madeley
Gay O'Mahoney
George McCaig
George Sandison
Georgia Panteli
Geraldine Brodie
Gill Saunders
Gilla Evans
Gillian Jondorf
Gillian Spencer
Gill Stern
Glynis Ellis
Graham Foster
Gregory August
    Raml

Hannes Heise
Helen Collins
Helen Weir
Helene Walters
Henriette Heise

Henrike Lähnemann
Howdy Reisdorf

Ian McAlister
Ian Mulder
Imogen Forster
Isabelle Kaufeler

Jane Whiteley
Janet Mullarney
Jeffery Collins
Jen Hamilton-Emery
Jennifer Cruickshank
Jennifer Higgins
Jennifer Hurstfield
Jenny Diski
Jerry Lynch
Jillian Jones
Joanne Hart
Joe Gill
Joel Love
Jon Lindsay Miles
Jonathan Evans
Jonathan Ruppin
Joseph Cooney
Joy Tobler
JP Sanders
Judith Unwin
Julia Sanches
Julian Duplain
Julian I Phillippi
Julie Van Pelt
Juraj Janik

K L Ee
Kaitlin Olson

Karan Deep Singh
Kasia Boddy
Kate Griffin
Kate Pullinger
Kate Wild
Katherine
    Wootton Joyce
Kathryn Lewis
Keith Dunnett
Kevin Acott
Kevin Brockmeier
Kevin Murphy
Kristin Djuve
Krystalli Glyniadakis

Larry Colbeck
Laura Bennett
Laura Jenkins
Laura Watkinson
Lauren Kassell
Lesley Lawn
Liam O'Connor
Linda Harte
Liz Clifford
Liz Tunnicliffe
Loretta Brown
Lorna Bleach
Lorna Scott Fox
Lucy Greaves
Lynda Graham

M Manfre
M C Hussey
Madeleine Kleinwort
Maggie Holmes
Maggie Peel

Margaret Jull Costa
Maria Pelletta
Marijke Du Toit
Marion Cole
Martin Brampton
Martin Conneely
Mary Nash
Matt Riggott
Matthew Bates
Matthew Francis
Michael Bagnall
Michael Harrison
Moira Fagan
Monika Olsen
Morgan Lyons
Murali Menon

N Jabinh
Nan Haberman
Natalie Rope
Natalie Smith
Natalie Wardle
Nichola Smalley
Nick Nelson
Nick Stevens
Nick Williams
Nuala Watt

Odhran Kelly
Oli Marlow
Owen Booth
Owen Fagan

P D Evans
Pamela Ritchie
Patrick Coyne

Paul Dowling
Paul Hannon
Paul Myatt
Peny Melmoth
Pete Ayrton
Peter Murray
Peter Vos
Philip Warren
Phyllis Reeve
Polly McLean
Poppy Toland

Quentin Webb

Rachel Eley
Rachel McNicholl
Rebecca K Morrison
Réjane Collard
Richard Jackson
Richard Soundy
Rob Fletcher
Rob Palk
Robert Gillett
Robert Leadbetter
Robin Woodburn
Ros Schwartz
Rosie Hedger
Ruth Martin

Samantha Schnee
Sean McGivern
Selin Kocagoz
Shazea Quraishi
Sheridan Marshall
Simon Pare
SLP

Sonia McLintock
Sophie Moreau
    Langlais
Steph Morris
Stephen Abbott
Stephen Bass
Stewart MacDonald
Sue Bradley
Sue Halpern
Sue Mckibben
Susana Medina

Tamsin Ballard
Tania Hershman
Tess Lee
Tess Lewis
Thomas Long
Thomas Fritz
Thomas Reedy
Tien Do
Tim Warren
Tom Russell
Tom Long
Tony Crofts
Tracey Martin
Tracy Northup

Vanessa Wells
Verena Weigert
Victoria Adams

Will Buck
William Buckingham

Zoe Brasier

Current & Upcoming Books by And Other Stories

Title: *Zbinden's Progress*
Author and Illustrator: Christoph Simon
Translator: Donal McLaughlin
Editor: Sophie Lewis
Proofreader: Wendy Toole
Typesetter: Alex Billington for Tetragon
Set in: Swift Neue Pro, Verlag
Series and Cover Design: Joseph Harries
Format: B Format with French flaps
Paper: Munken Premium Cream 80gsm FSC
Printer: T J International Ltd, Padstow, Cornwall

FSC
www.fsc.org
MIX
Paper from
responsible sources
FSC® C013056